An

EncouragingU

Christmas

David + Lynn,

Thank you for your support –

May you find encouragement in these pages –

Doug Cr—

Doug Creamer

Ann Farabee

Lynna Clark

Roger Barbee

David Freeze

An EncouragingU Christmas

Doug Creamer, Ann Farabee, Lynna Clark

Roger Barbee, David Freeze

Copyright © 2020

Cover design by M. D. Cox

Published by Faith Farm Publishing Company

PO Box 777

Faith, NC 28041

Scripture quotations marked (NLT) are taken from the Holy Bible, New Living Translation, copyright ©1996, 2004, 2015 by Tyndale House Foundation. Used by permission of Tyndale House Publishers, a Division of Tyndale House Ministries, Carol Stream, Illinois 60188. All rights reserved.

Some Scripture taken from the HOLY BIBLE, NEW INTERNATIONAL VERSION. Copyright 1973, 1978, 1984 International Bible Society. Used by permission of Zondervan Bible Publishers.

Some Scripture taken from the Holy Bible, King James Version

Some of the material in this book is based on material that has appeared elsewhere in another form.

ISBN: 978-0-9743935-5-1

FORWARD

An idea is conceived: About a year ago Lynna Clark sent me the story you will find in this book. She said I could use it however I thought. I considered putting it on the website but felt it deserved something more. So, like many things in life, I set it aside.

Summer rolled around and this wonderful story just wouldn't quit nagging me that it needed some attention. What was I supposed to do with it? I was digging through a drawer and found a copy of a story that I wrote titled, "Tommy's Christmas." The version I found is nothing like the version that appears here, because it needed lots of work. It was summer. Who wants to work on a Christmas story in summer? But wait a minute…the idea was born!

I emailed Lynna and shared the idea. She gave me the big thumbs up. After getting approval from the other contributors to the book, excitement began to build. We would put a book together! I started the rewrite of my story and found it started to flow very well. The others started pulling and writing material and sending it in. The idea was growing up.

I go to church with a young artist. I shared the idea with him. "Would you be interested in creating a cover?" The answer won't surprise you. The idea gets a little bigger.

We've all been working hard to bring this idea to full maturity. What you are holding is the result of all of our efforts. Our hope and desire is that you be blessed and encouraged as you read. We also hope that you will help us spread the word, not only about the book but also about the website: www.EncouragingU.com/

CONTENTS

My most special childhood Christmas traditions

By David Freeze

I grew up on a large tract of land centered around a small dairy farm. In the beginning, I thought everybody must be just like me. Lots of land for play and exploration, and yes plenty of work to be done. We began doing our chores as small kids and even that usually seemed like fun. Lots of cows and a couple horses made me happy. Happy even when we got up before school and went to milk those cows by hand, hours before the school bell would ring.

We had plenty of food and lots of it came from the farm. I thought everybody must have a full refrigerator and freezer jammed with meats and vegetables. And shelves full of home canned goods. We did all that in the summer with a huge garden. In fact, all these things happened in the summer. I loved the summer, especially shorts and bare feet.

But my favorite day of the year was during winter. Still is, nothing tops Christmas day! I treasured everything about it. Cold didn't bother me then and our family had favorite traditions that I've never forgotten. Leading up to Christmas Day in a small house, increasing amounts of decorations and smells of the season filled my senses. As one of three kids, I loved sharing the work of putting up those decorations and making cookies and candy. My mom was a great cook, and I was a better than average eater, especially for those precisely cut out sugar cookies. It seemed that every afternoon,

3

headed home from school or inside from our farm work, I longed to cover myself with the warmth and smells of the season's many special treats.

Two really big traditions stood out, seemingly never missed at Christmastime throughout my childhood. The first involved a rifle and a shotgun. I always remember a special adventure perfect for a chilly Saturday morning. Just a week or so ahead of the big day itself, my dad walked my brother and me to the deepest woods we had, as far away from the house as we could go. Sometimes along the way, we looked for rabbits and squirrels, but the main target was mistletoe. I was never a good shot, but my dad and brother were. All we wanted to do was a fill a small bag with the green mistletoe, realizing a bonus if there were berries on it. Imagine a small boy with a gun shooting towards a green clump that seemed so high up in a huge tree. My dad could hit the clumps with a rifle and drop a bundle without holes through the little leaves. I usually could not and got to try with a shotgun. Pointing the shotgun so high almost guaranteed a bruised shoulder the next day but that was OK. I dropped some usually and felt especially good to later decorate using those leaves with small holes, knowing they were mine. I remember taking some of the best to church to give away, realizing that most of the other families didn't get the adventure of mistletoe hunting.

My second and always best tradition also came even closer to Christmas, never more than just a few days ahead. Our Christmas tree always came from somewhere on the farm. I remember a certain field that always had plenty of well-shaped cedars. Not quite as far away as the mistletoe woods, we carried an axe or a hatchet and went in search of the perfect tree. Sometimes my sister walked along but always one of the boys got to chop the tree down. No chain saws allowed, so once the tree was found, we made quick work of cutting it.

Then came the long walk back to the house, when dragging the tree was just another honor. I imagine I dragged the tree more than I cut it, but either one was OK. Any part of this was exciting for me, especially as a small child. This was our tree and my treasured symbol of the greatest day of the year.

Back at the house, my dad used a hand saw to cut the base of the tree off clean and straight, then nailed a couple of boards together on the bottom so that it would stand up. Watering the tree wasn't needed since Christmas by then was only a day or two away. Christmas was centered in the living room of the house and the tree found its regular spot, not far but just enough from the fireplace. Big and colorful lights, a coating of washing detergent snow and silver icicles, then eventually topped by a star, we had a tree. A small white blanket covered the boards, making the floor underneath ready for presents.

Someone plugged in the lights and Christmas, my favorite day of the year, was just ahead. The cedar smell proved it!

This Season

By Lynna Clark

Currently we have three local grandchildren, all seven years old. I had the bright idea to host a sleep-over a few weeks back so their parents could have date nights. The kids get along great so I wasn't worried at all about them. But my old bones do not function like they used to. Right now I'm going through a season of pain. I knew it would be hard to keep up.

At bedtime we put the two boy cousins in the guest room and our granddaughter was given the privilege of sleeping with her grandmother. David was blessed with the recliner. I think he was happy to make the "sacrifice." After much giggling, adjusting of covers, lanterns and flashlights I passed out on my side of the bed. The next morning everyone was up and at 'em long before me. David had the kids at the breakfast table as I toddled that way. When I came around the corner I heard sweet Marie say, as if sharing a secret, "Did y'all know Grammy snores?"

"HEY!" I startled her. "You're not supposed to rat out your Grammy!"

The three of them laughed and began saying how next time they were going to switch places. It seemed nobody wanted to sleep with Grammy. Jesse looked at me with pity, moved from his place and put his arm around me.

"I'll sleep with you Grammy," he said in a sympathetic tone. Marie held her ground. But Able noticed and came to me as well.

Hoping my feelings weren't hurt, he too promised. "I'll sleep with you Grammy."

Jesse piped up. "You first!"

I thought David might snort Aldi-O's through his nose.

These kids. They bring me so much joy. Seven short years ago we wondered if God would ever hear our prayers for little ones. Able was due to arrive the following May, but his brother Aven had died before birth. We had reason to be afraid when Able was born ten weeks early.

Our youngest daughter and her husband had been on the adoption waiting list so long that they had to go through another home study. That fall God saw fit to bless their home with two babies at once; a boy and a girl, three weeks apart.

Seven years ago at Christmas our home was quiet… well, except for the snoring. That's been a lifelong… situation. There was no pitter-patter of little feet. There were no hand-crafted fingerprint gifts made for the mamas. I had no reason to count batteries or shop for Legos and Lite-Brites. But now!

Oh be still my heart! Everyone's fighting over who gets to sleep with Grammy!

Maybe this season for you is not so jolly and bright. Perhaps this is not the most wonderful time of the year in your world. May I offer a word of hope?

Speak to the Lord the longing of your soul. Cast all your care on Him, for He cares for you. Then watch as He brings you through this season and into the next. He alone is faithful and true.

Just remember that His timing is always wiser than ours. So many things had to work out before we got our little ones. And this mystery illness still plagues me though we've begged Him for years to take it away. The pain grows greater each passing day. Yet I know He hears the longing of my heart and will continue to bless us "in due season, if we faint not."

"He that spared not His own Son, but delivered Him up for us all, how shall He not with Him freely give us all things?"

May the Lord bless you and keep you in His wonderful care, no matter the season you're in.

Resources:
Galatians 6:9; Romans 8:32; 1 Peter 5:7(NLT)

Christmas Traditions

By Doug Creamer

I was talking with a friend recently about things that people do traditionally at Christmas. There are so many traditions that people develop at this time of year. The things that our families did when we were all young make up an important part of the things we want to do each year.

A friend told me that he and his sister exchange gag gifts which is a fun part of their Christmas tradition. I remember going to many Christmas parties where everyone brought something and then you took turns opening up something from under the tree. You could also steal other people's presents, which made the game fun. The best gifts make the rounds all night long. There is always so much laughter and everyone seems to have fun getting or stealing the best presents.

Many people begin the Christmas season with the tradition of putting up the Christmas tree and decorating the outside of their house on Thanksgiving weekend. In our community people like to decorate the outside of their homes. Some people go classic with the greenery and the lights in the windows. Others enjoy putting up lots of lights on and around the house. Several of my neighbors have the inflatable yard decorations while others have the animated characters. Several of my neighbors have the holy family displayed in their yards.

Many people's Christmas traditions are centered on food and special treats. My brother's family makes cookies and fudge and then they make up plates to take to their neighbors. My mother-in-law loves to cook all kinds of delectable treats for Christmas. She makes pies, cakes, cookies and the biggest Christmas feast you can imagine. My mother always has plenty of cookies around but the family favorite has to be her pumpkin bread. I can't imagine Christmas without it.

The best tradition of Christmas has to be going to the Christmas Eve service. I love going to church on Christmas Eve because everything is done. I can finally stop, breath, and really contemplate the reason for the season. I love to hear the Christmas story and to hear a pastor reflect on the meaning of such a holy night. Most of all I think I love to sing the beautiful Christmas carols. I don't need the hymnal; I know most of them by heart. Some years I had a hard time finding a church that had a Christmas service.

One time my little sister and I were talking about the Christmas Eve service at the church we attended when I was growing up. I told her that I loved each year when this one woman would sing a solo of O Holy Night. When she sang that song, it seemed to signal to my soul the arrival of the Christ child. My sister told me that for her it was when this gentleman sang Sweet Little Jesus Boy. She said she knew when he sang that Christmas had finally come.

There are so many wonderful traditions that go with this time of year, but I hope that you will find a way to slow the pace of life down long enough to spend some quiet moments in a church thinking about what Jesus did for you and thanking Him for being willing to leave heaven and to come to earth for you. Christmas is a personal thing for God. He paid the highest price He could to have a relationship with you and me. God wanted it so bad that He sent His son into the world to take away our sin.

Christmas wouldn't be Christmas without all the wonderful traditions, but we have to be careful to make sure the traditions don't overshadow the purpose. Jesus didn't come in a palace where only the royalty could touch and know Him. He came in a manger so He could reach out to all mankind. He came to reveal to us God's love and forgiveness, gifts that are far greater than any you'll find under your Christmas tree.

I want to encourage you to carve out a little bit of time before the big day arrives and reflect on God's reason for this wonderful season. God loves you and He even likes you just the way you are. He wants you to get to know Him, His Son, and the Holy Spirit. He wants you to experience His perfect love which casts out all fear. Reflecting on these things should become a part of your Christmas traditions. I hope this final week of preparation for the coming of Christ is a good one for you.

A Son is Given

By Lynna Clark

Prologue

It's a miracle they married. Both were terribly shy. When he turned eighteen, his father Jacob began reminding him often that it was time to take a wife and add to the family. Good sturdy sons would help expand the carpentry business. Joseph smiled and nodded. He and his father already had someone in mind… if Joseph could just get up the nerve.

The thought of her warmed him. She was quiet and pretty and reminded him of a doe, tentatively checking her surroundings as if afraid of being noticed. Though they'd been raised in the same small village, their times of interaction had been too scarce for Joseph's liking. He wished for an opportunity to draw her aside and express his feelings.

Finally one morning in the marketplace it happened. He'd made an excuse to be there hoping to see her. She was startled when he purposely bumped into her knocking the figs from her basket. Quickly they bent toward the ground together to retrieve the fruit before it was trampled.

"Forgive me Mary! Let me get those for you." Joseph tried to appear unruffled just like he'd practiced in his head. He was rewarded with a shy smile. Mary looked up and tried to think of something to say.

"What brings you to the market today Josey?"

He was pleased that she used his boyhood name and decided to just go for it.

"Why you dear Mary! I was hoping to see you!"

Mary blushed as she tried to gather herself. Though she was veiled Joseph could tell he'd embarrassed her. Quietly he continued.

"I know that your father is not well. But do you think he is strong enough to receive visitors?"

Mary was surprised and blushed even deeper. Her reply took so long that Joseph's heart pounded while he waited.

"Yes," she finally managed. Again she looked into the eyes of her childhood friend. His gentleness had always comforted her when other young men seemed boisterous and proud. Suddenly it occurred to her how much she liked him. Hopefully he would speak to her father soon as there had been another suitor who had visited a few days earlier. Thankfully she had sent him away since her father had been too weak that day. She smiled to herself and silently thanked the Lord for His kindness. Joseph's gentle question broke into her thoughts.

"Should I wait until he feels better?"

Mary was alarmed. If Joseph waited the other suitor might win her father's favor. Though Simon was financially well off and highly regarded amongst the temple rulers, he was also rather arrogant. She had a feeling her status as his wife would be somewhat of a business transaction.

But Joseph...

She realized the man still waited for her reply. When her eyes met his she knew. "Please come at your earliest convenience. My father grows weaker each day and he will be thankful to receive you."

Joseph was encouraged. Though she bowed slightly and moved away, her glance back at him gave wings to his feet. There was urgency in her request that seemed to be about more than her father's health.

Joseph hurried home to speak to his own father. God willing, he would pursue this gentle girl before the sun set in the Nazareth sky.

Chapter One

When Mary returned home she was surprised to find Simon talking with her father. Plus he'd brought gifts; extravagant ones: fine jewelry, wine, lovely clothes and of course a contract. Her father seemed thrilled to share the news.

"Our friend Simon has come to ask if he may seek your hand in marriage. I assured him you would welcome his generous offer. Shall we proceed with the betrothal ceremony my daughter?"

Mary wondered how to answer without breaking her father's heart. He had expressed many times his desire to see her betrothed before his life ended.

But Simon was not her first love.

With resolve she looked at Simon. His clothing confirmed his wealth and she wondered why he'd chosen her, a simple peasant girl. It would be a huge insult to reject his proposal.

"Forgive me my lord. I must decline your offer. There is another in my life who has expressed his intentions before you. But I shall forever be thankful for your kindness and generosity."

Apparently Simon was not accustomed to rejection. His face turned bright red and his expression changed immediately. Instead of his normal look of confidence, he now wore a smirk. An insult lingered on the tip of his tongue but Mary saved him from it.

"Please accept my gratitude. The gifts you brought are exquisite. It pains me to return such treasure." She closed the beautiful box containing the garnet necklace and ring. As she placed the box in his hand she bowed without looking into his eyes.

Saying nothing, he gathered his lavish gifts, turned on his heel and exited the small home.

Mary's father sat heavily on his bed and began to cough. She fetched water and sat beside him stroking his back. Though his cough calmed, he said nothing.

She whispered in the old man's ear.

"I love you dear Abba. But Simon is not the man for me. The Lord our God is mighty! He will provide."

Old Heli took his daughter's hand. The girl always amazed him with her strength. Though it would have relieved his worry to have her betrothed to a man of wealth and high standing, he was strangely comforted that she turned Simon away. Perhaps like him, his daughter would marry for love.

Chapter Two

Her only sister had married and moved to the home of her husband a few years earlier. The Lord had already blessed the couple with a son and a daughter. Since Mary's mother had passed away, the care of her father was left in her hands. Mary adored the old man and suspected his ill health was due to the loss of his wife. Such love was shared between them that she longed for the same. The family had been through many hardships and had always struggled to keep food on the table. But their meager home was filled with joy. Having no sons, Heli was determined to teach his daughters the Word of God. Mary was his best student and daily sat at his feet soaking in the beautiful words. Her favorite came from the Psalms as her father often chose to sing them to her.

"Are you strong enough to bless me with a song tonight dear Abba?"

Heli looked at his innocent daughter and wondered if she realized the grand life she had turned away earlier in the day. He also wondered about the other suitor she referred to when she refused Simon's offer.

"How can I say no to such a beautiful girl? Which would you like to hear?"

Mary smiled as she requested one of her favorites. "Sing to me a song of our father David. The one that starts with 'Let all that I am praise the LORD; with my whole heart, I will praise His holy Name!'"

Heli joined her and together they continued.

"Let all that I am praise the LORD; may I never forget the good things He does for me. He forgives all my sins and heals all my diseases. He redeems me from death and crowns me with love and tender mercies. He fills my life with good things. My youth is renewed like the eagle's!"

Mary gazed at her father and was happy to see that his smile had returned as well as a measure of strength while they sang the beautiful song. They continued with vigor and she smiled brightly when they came to the lovely words.

"The Lord is like a father to his children, tender and compassionate to those who fear Him. For He knows how weak we are; He remembers we are only dust. Our days on earth are like grass; like wildflowers, we bloom and die. The wind blows and we are gone- as though we had never been here. But the love of the LORD remains forever with those who fear Him. His salvation extends to the children's children of those who are faithful to His covenant, of those who obey his commandments!"

She paused as though she couldn't remember the next lines so that she could enjoy the voice of her father. Heartily he continued.

"The LORD has made the heavens His throne; from there He rules over everything. Praise the LORD, you angels, you mighty ones who carry out His plans, listening for each of His commands. Yes praise the LORD, you armies of angels who serve Him and do His will. Praise the LORD, everything He has created, everything in all His kingdom!"

Mary joined him with beautiful harmony on the last line.

"Let all that I am praise the LORD!"

Their voices could be heard through the door where Joseph and his father stood listening to the wonderful psalm. The lovely girl he had teased in his youth was hopefully about to become his wife.

16

Chapter Three

The soft knock on the door caused Mary's heart to flutter. To her delight it was Joseph with his father Jacob. "Is Heli well enough to receive us?"

Joseph was happy when Mary ushered them inside. "Yes! He is feeling the strength of a soaring eagle! Come! Would you like something to eat?"

Joseph was glad that she seemed to relax in her own home. He felt a bit more at ease there too. But he hesitated to eat lest he choke before asking the question.

"A little water would be nice."

Mary smiled at his gentle request as she noticed again his timidity. "Of course! Father, this is my friend Joseph and his father Jacob. Do you remember Josey from our youth?"

Heli nodded knowingly. The young man had shot up like a tender reed. Joseph, though a few years older than the girls, had often walked Mary and her sister home as the three of them grew up together.

"Yes, come sit with me! Mary brought fresh fruit from the market today and blessed this old man with delicious fig cakes. Just like Abigail brought to David, they are fit for a king! Sit my friends and have some!"

Mary smiled at her father's enthusiasm and served their guests. Joseph relaxed a little more and took a bite. "Oh!" he exclaimed. "As you so accurately said, fit for a king!" He sipped his water and silently summoned the Almighty for strength.

The room became quiet for longer than any of them liked. Jacob wondered how long it would take his son to broach the subject as he had asked to handle the matter himself. Without saying a word, Joseph stood as if leaving. Mary's heart dropped and old Heli wondered how to help. Still saying nothing Joseph stepped outside for a breath of fresh air. Heli stole a glance at his kindhearted daughter and saw her disappointment. She obviously had deep affection for the young man.

Before any of them could speak, Joseph returned. Slowly he presented the mohar to Heli: wedding coins, a marriage contract plus a skin of wine. Humbly Joseph bowed. "I've come to ask for your daughter Mary to be my wife."

With tears of joy, old Heli looked toward Mary. She smiled and nodded her approval.

Joseph then offered his gift to Mary. "I made this for you. I hope to fill it with treasure someday."

Mary received the box and admired the intricate carvings. "Oh Josey! I can think of nothing I would like more than a gift made by your own hand. It's beautiful!"

Heli smiled as he observed young Joseph. "I have very little to offer, but what I have is yours. Will you dear Mary be my wife?"

Mary looked at her father. "May we have your blessing Abba?"

Heli and Jacob stood, embraced their children, then each other. Once Heli found his voice he pronounced a blessing on the union which of course included a prayer for many children.

"You have made an old man very happy Joseph! I know you will be good to my daughter. May the Lord bless you and keep you my son. Now for the wine!" He poured from the wineskin Joseph brought. When the four of them shared wine, the betrothal was sealed. Through her veil, Joseph gazed into Mary's kind and beautiful eyes. He was more convinced than ever that he had chosen well.

"Please accept this ring as my pledge. I am yours and you are mine. Many waters cannot quench love, nor can rivers drown it."

She repeated the words in sweet agreement as they dreamed of their future together. "I accept this ring and pledge the same. I am yours and you are mine. Many waters cannot quench love, nor can rivers drown it."

Joseph placed a ring on the index finger of Mary's right hand for the world to see. This beautiful girl he had loved since his youth was officially pledged to be his wife.

"I go to my father's house to prepare a home that we may dwell together as husband and wife. Behold you are consecrated unto me with this ring according to the laws of Moses and Israel. I promise to be faithful, to love and protect you all the days of my life."

Mary smiled knowing that his promises were true.

Jacob signed the contract and gave it to Heli for safe keeping. The two proud fathers shared another embrace knowing their children had chosen well.

Joseph drew Mary aside as he prepared to leave.

"You are lovely tonight my bride. My brothers are all envious and have warned me to get our home built quickly lest you back out of such a humble offer."

Mary shook her head. "Never dear Josey! I am my beloved's and you are mine. Many waters cannot quench love."

Joseph kissed the ring on her finger. "I will miss you my doe. I have assigned our brother Abel to watch over you until I come. So be ready! I will be back for you sooner than you think!"

Mary gazed into the eyes of her groom. "May everything be according to your word!"

Chapter Four

Mary rose early the next morning and walked the short distance across the village to her sister's home. She shared the news and the two young women hugged as they considered raising their families together. Traditionally a groom took twelve months to complete the home. Then he would gather his companions, shout to announce his coming, and collect his bride.

"I hope Joseph doesn't plan a long betrothal. Father grows weaker each day. I'd love to hear him speak a blessing on our wedding day."

Suzanna teased, "Not to mention, the sooner you two get started the closer our children will be!"

Mary laughed and blushed a little. "I've always thought so much of Joseph. His family is almost as poor as ours, but he is such a gentleman. Did you know he assigned your husband Abel as my guardian?"

Suzanna sighed. "No! The man tells me nothing! Just wait until he returns this evening!" The sisters shared a laugh then Mary continued. "Simon also stopped by yesterday. I couldn't look at him though father was delighted at his offer. If he only knew how forward the man is, he would not have been so eager to invite Simon into my life."

Suzanna caught her breath as she expressed concern for her little sister. "Mary! You turned that rascal away? Surely you know he will not give up easily!"

Mary shook her head. "I have no idea why he would want a peasant girl like me anyway. Women flock to his wealth and power. I would rather live in a stable than to share his bed." She shivered at the thought.

Her sister laughed. "If you marry Joseph, you may just get your wish. I had a feeling Joseph would ask. He's looked at you like a lovesick schoolboy for years."

Mary smiled. "I'm afraid I've looked at him the same. I just never knew that he noticed until yesterday."

"Of course he noticed! You my little sister are beautiful! THAT is why Simon seeks you. No one matches your beauty whether rich or poor. I'm glad you refused him! But please be careful. I've heard terrible things about him. He did not rise to such power and wealth through kindness. In fact, as pleasant as our visit has been, let's get you packed and on your way home before it grows any later."

Chapter Five

As strong and vibrant as Heli was for the betrothal ceremony, Mary took hope that perhaps he was recovering. He spoke often of her and Joseph's future and seemed to relish telling stories of his own marriage. Mary loved their time together and grew hopeful that perhaps her beloved Abba would live to see her wedding day.

But it was not to be.

She returned from the market several months later to find that dear Heli gasped for air. She held his hand and tried to smile. "Rest in the words of our father David my beloved Abba.

'The LORD is my shepherd, I shall not want. He makes me lie down in green pastures; He leads me beside still waters; He restores my soul. He leads me in paths of righteousness for His Name's sake. Even though I walk through the valley of the shadow of death, I will fear no evil, for Thou art with me; Thy rod and Thy staff, they comfort me. You prepare a table before me in the presence of my enemies. You anoint my head with oil; my cup overflows. Surely goodness and mercy will follow me all the days of my life, and I will dwell in the house of the LORD forever.'"

Gazing beyond his daughter to the God he had humbly served for a lifetime, Heli smiled and breathed his last. Peace flooded his old soul as he shed his earthly tent and joined the wife of his youth. Though the light in his eyes was gone, the smile on his lips told the truth. He was free from the chains of suffering and pain.

Mary sobbed into her father's chest but whispered a prayer of thanksgiving that he no longer struggled for air.

As was customary, Heli was washed and prepared for burial that same day then placed in the family tomb. Mary's grief was nearly unbearable though she was surrounded by friends and neighbors. Joseph grieved her loss but felt ashamed for his own unhappiness. He knew his sadness was more about postponing the wedding than losing Heli. Though it had been three months since the betrothal, he must now wait at least a year to claim his bride.

"Take heart my son!" Jacob tried to encourage him. "She will be your wife forever! This gives us more time to make your new home something very special."

Joseph nodded and busied himself with his work. His father was right. Mary had lived such a meager life. With his father's help he could provide a home worthy of her.

While Joseph threw himself into his work he remembered a story of long ago. Another Jacob, son of Isaac, had labored seven long years for Rachel. After his wedding night he discovered he had been given her sister Leah. Jacob worked seven more years to obtain his true love. Joseph sighed and thanked the Almighty that Mary's only sister was already married.

He shook the thought from his head. No man should try to please two women!

But sweet Mary...

He smiled at the thought of her as he remembered the line from the Torah about Jacob. "Though he worked seven years for her, his love was so strong that it seemed but a moment."

Joseph determined to do the same. No matter how long it took, nor whatever the circumstances, his love for Mary would overcome it all.

Chapter Six

For Mary the days passed slowly. Meals of consolation from friends and neighbors poured in for seven days. Suzanna and her husband kept Mary company the first week of mourning then returned home. Suddenly she realized how alone she felt. Everything reminded Mary of her father and mother. Her parents had so faithfully taught her the Word of God that most evenings were spent recalling their favorite passages. Night after night she found herself lying in bed crying out those same words to the Lord.

She longed for comfort and thought of Joseph. Though there were only three months left in the bereavement period, she wondered if she could endure that long. Her sadness was overwhelming. She listened for his shout every evening just in case he decided to come early. But knowing Joseph he would respect the tradition of grieving the loss of a parent for twelve months. His family was all about honor, tradition, and protecting the family name.

That was part of her attraction to him. Joseph was indeed a very good man.

She readied herself for bed and turned in early. The sun had not even set but she didn't care. The cupboards were as empty as her soul. It mattered not as she had lost her appetite weeks ago.

A knock came at the door. Mary was startled and checked before answering.

No one was there.

Carefully she looked again. A basket filled with delicacies had been placed by the door. As she brought the wonderful food inside she wondered who would be so kind. She smiled at the thought of Joseph. Surely it was him.

She peered through the door again but failed to see the man in the shadows. With the latch returned to its place, she carried the basket to the table. There was enough food to last for over a week! She praised God not only for His provision, but also that she would have no need to leave her home for days.

Except for Joseph, she preferred solitude. It seemed the Almighty was preparing her soul for something ahead. A favorite Psalm came to mind so she sang it out loud.

"The LORD is like a Father to His children, tender and compassionate to those who fear Him. For He knows how weak we are; He remembers we are only dust."

Chapter Seven

As Joseph walked toward home he hoped the gift would comfort his fiancée. He knew from her sister that Mary was lonely and terribly sad. He considered speaking to his father about the possibility of bringing her home to wed before the bereavement period was over. As her husband he could comfort her and make sure she was cared for. Perhaps the Lord would bless them with a child right away. They could name him Heli after her father and honor his good name.

Joseph walked a bit faster as he thought on his plan. The house he prepared for Mary was complete except for a few last minute touches. His father had diligently helped him add the new rooms to the family home. He would understand and might even support Joseph breaking tradition.

But his mother…

Joseph shivered a little. She would not be pleased. The wedding feast was a really big deal to her and she had much left to prepare. In fact she seemed glad to have more time to gather everything needed for the upcoming celebration. Since Joseph was the youngest of her sons it would be her last wedding feast to host.

As Joseph thought on everything he decided to do what was best for Mary. The sight of her as she answered her door had made him happy. But then she had looked up, searching for the gift giver. Her lovely face was drawn and sad. Joseph felt an urgent need to take care of her like never before. His mother would have to understand. Perhaps his father would help with that.

Joseph breathed a prayer for Mary as he made his way home.

"As our father Moses said: 'Give us gladness in proportion to our former misery! Replace the evil years with good. Let us, Your servants, see You work again; let our children see Your glory. And may the Lord our God show us His approval, and make our efforts successful. Yes, make our efforts successful!'"

Chapter Eight

Mary enjoyed a fig cake and thought of her betrothal day. Her father had been so happy. She looked at the simple ring on her finger and recalled dear Joseph as he asked her to be his bride. Peace flooded her soul and she thanked the Almighty for His kindness and comfort.

As she put the food away, suddenly the small room was filled with warmth and light. A very large man stood before her. Mary's heart pounded as she took in his presence.

"Greetings favored woman! The Lord is with you!"

She gazed at the heavenly being and realized her mouth was open. Her heart still pounded as she thought on his words and tried to understand what he meant. Though he was obviously powerful she marveled at his gentleness when he spoke again. "Don't be afraid Mary, for you have found favor with God."

There was that word again. What had she done to gain favor? The angel continued.

"You will conceive and give birth to a Son and you will name Him Jesus. He will be very great and will be called the Son of the Most High. The Lord God will give Him the throne of His ancestor David. And He will reign over Israel forever; His Kingdom will never end!"

Mary thought on the words then finally found her voice. She blushed as she asked the obvious. "But... how, how can this happen... since, I am a virgin?"

The angel softly replied, "The Holy Spirit will come upon you and the power of the Most High will overshadow you. So the Baby to be born will be holy, and He will be called the Son of God."

Mary sat down. Her head was spinning. The angel waited as if allowing her to take it all in. Quietly he continued. "What's more, your relative Elizabeth is going to have a child in her old age! People used to say she was barren, but she has conceived a son and is now in her sixth month."

The angel smiled broadly when he added. "For nothing is impossible with God!"

Mary returned his smile and joy flooded her soul.

"I am the Lord's servant! May everything you have said about me come true!"

The angel disappeared as quickly as he had come. Mary was left alone with her thoughts while she searched her memory for Scripture about the Messiah.

Chapter Nine

When Joseph arrived home he was disappointed to find his father occupied with the family meal. His brothers gathered around the table laughing and talking. His mother greeted him with a hug as well as a scolding.

"Where were you my son? I was beginning to worry!"

Joseph kissed his mother's cheek as he caught the eye of his father. They shared a smile knowing her question was more about gaining information than real concern. The woman struggled to let go of her youngest though he was most certainly a grown man.

"Dear woman, I was delivering a basket of supplies to Mary. She is going through a very difficult time you know. Though her father passed nearly nine months ago she is still very sad."

Joseph's mother eyed him curiously. "And how do you know her condition? It is not permitted for you to visit her alone!"

Joseph's brothers laughed heartily at that. But with one look their mother silenced them. Joseph assured his mother.

"Abel sought me out so that I would know she does not fare well. I gathered a few things for Mary and left them by her door. We did not even speak."

His mother noticed Joseph's sadness and determined to comfort him with a huge helping of food. "Come! Eat! Her time of grief will be over in three short months and there is still much to do! You would be wise to fill your belly with good food while you can. Mary is much too beautiful to know how to cook properly!"

Joseph laughed at his mother's attempt to comfort him, especially when she realized she had just insulted her other daughters-in-law. Feisty Miriam spoke up with mischief.

"Thankfully I am so ugly my husband will never go hungry!"

At that the family laughed and relaxed around their evening meal.

Chapter Ten

The moment she closed her eyes she fell into a wonderful peaceful rest. In her dreams she recalled Adam's deep sleep as God removed a rib to form the woman who would complete him. Mary smiled and thought on the goodness of God. Throughout history young women had dreamed of bringing the Messiah into the world to save their people. For some unknown reason, she had found favor and would bear His Son.

When she woke she knew exactly what to do. Quickly she packed and headed to her sister's home. Suzanna's husband Abel was just leaving and was surprised to see Mary.

"You're out early today little one! And you look like you're on a mission. Are you feeling better?"

Mary smiled. "Yes! I've decided to visit our Aunt Elizabeth for a while. Can you make sure Joseph knows so he doesn't worry?"

Abel tipped his head. He was concerned for this young woman he'd grown to love as his sister. "I will… but are you sure you want to travel so far? It's nearly time for your wedding."

Mary nodded. "There are three months left to grieve for father. I should be back by the end of that time. Judea is only a five day journey."

Abel hesitated. "Surely you have traveling companions…"

Suzanna came from the house with a baby on one hip and a toddler clinging to her skirt. "Catch me up sister. You're going where?" Mary hoped her sister wouldn't detect the joy she found hard to contain. Suzanna was always the best at dragging secrets from her soul.

"I feel the Lord wants me to spend time with Aunt Elizabeth. She is so dear and she's certainly not getting any younger. Besides, it's still three months until the wedding and I'm not doing well in the old house without father."

Suzanna gazed at her younger sibling intently. She was sure the girl was hiding something. Trying to get more information she asked, "Does Joseph know you are going? He's not going with you is he?"

Mary was shocked. "No! Of course not! I haven't spoken to Josey. But Abel has promised to let him know where I am. Now, I must be on my way if I'm going to catch up with the caravan headed to Judea."

Chapter Eleven

Mary kissed her sister and headed toward the town square. She looked through the crowd hoping she would know some of the other travelers. Though she had made the trip before, it had always included her father. Suddenly fear gripped her heart. At least she had provision for the journey thanks to Joseph.

She wished very much to speak to him before she left. Her beautiful secret would certainly involve him too. As she made her way through the people a thousand thoughts filled her mind.

"In the multitude of my thoughts within me Lord, Thy comforts delight my soul."

Trying to be brave she whispered, "Guide me O Thou great Jehovah!"

Somehow she bumped right into him.

"Josey!" she laughed at the look on his face.

He motioned her to the side under a sycamore tree where they could speak face to face. "Sweet Mary! What brings you into town on the busiest day of the week? And why do you carry so many bags?" He began taking things from her shoulders trying to help.

She could hardly keep from reaching out to him. This dear man meant everything to her, yet she had no idea how he would react to the news.

Mary placed the rest of her supplies on the ground beside her and silently asked the Lord for help. "Joseph, I need to visit my Aunt Elizabeth right away. But I'll be back in three months. I promise!"

Joseph grew somber and looked into her eyes. "You're going all the way to the Judean hill country? What's the matter? Has old Zechariah finally passed?"

Mary shook her head. "No, I think he's... doing very well!"

She wondered how much to say. Then she realized. Her news would have to come out sometime. Joseph might as well be the first to know.

She sat down on one of her bags. Joseph took a seat on the wooden crate in front of her. He could tell she struggled but he was not prepared for what she said next. "Joseph, I had an angel visit last night." Mary peered into his eyes trying to read him. Joseph tipped his head slightly but said nothing. Mary slowly continued.

"He said he'd been sent by God to let me know..."

She couldn't say the words.

Joseph interrupted her thoughts.

"Did you eat too much garlic and gefilte fish before bedtime? That stuff can make you have all kinds of crazy dreams. Don't go running off to Judea to your old Aunt Elizabeth. God has not even blessed them with children so something's not right in that household. I know you're grieving, but I've spoken to my father and if you're willing, we can break tradition and get married before the bereavement period is over. I want to take care of you! And I sure can't do that if you're half a countryside away!"

Mary glanced past Joseph to make sure the caravan didn't leave without her. She felt the nudging in her soul to get it over with. It must be said.

"Joseph, stop. It was a real angel… huge! He informed me that Aunt Elizabeth has conceived in her old age and will bear a son in three months. I'm going to help her. And…"

Mary realized she had Joseph's attention.

"I have been chosen to bear the Son of God… our Messiah!"

Joseph hardly knew what to say. Quietly he whispered. "Oh Mary! How wonderful! Should we get married right away? I mean, obviously the Almighty knows we are betrothed!"

Mary teared up and struggled to speak. The words of the angel explained it best so when they came back to her she repeated them to Joseph.

"The angel said I will conceive and give birth to a Son and name Him Jesus. When I asked him how that could happen since I am a virgin, he said 'The Holy Spirit will come upon you and the power of the Most High will overshadow you. So the Baby to be born will be holy, and He will be called the Son of God.'"

She looked at Joseph as she added. "It seems important that I remain a virgin until after the baby is born. There is a prophecy in the book of Isaiah which promises a Son of the Most High Who will be born of a virgin. I don't know how… or when… I just know enough to say yes to the Almighty."

The reality of what his fiancée had spoken finally hit him. This would not be his son.

He couldn't speak.

A commotion down the street caught their attention. Mary stood and began gathering her things. "I'm sorry Josey. I have to go. But I'll be back soon!" She smiled tentatively and tried to get him to look at her. But he wouldn't.

Instead he finished gathering her things and walked with her to the manager of the caravan. As he pulled coins from his pouch and handed them to the man he added, "Take good care of her please. Good-bye Mary."

Joseph turned and walked away without looking back. His heart was broken. Apparently Mary had been unfaithful and this was her way of covering the truth. No wonder she had stayed ill so many months after her father's passing.

There had been another.

Chapter Twelve

Since she still wore the clothing of bereavement it did not seem unusual for the young woman to shed tears.

There were many.

Mary knew she was being treated especially courteous by those traveling with her. She recognized some from her hometown but appreciated the caravan leader most of all. He and his wife seemed to take Joseph's words to heart. In less than a week she gained safe passage to the Judean hills where her relatives made their home.

But her heart was with Joseph. She wondered if she had lost him forever. What man would believe the words she had spoken? Plus his good-bye had seemed so final.

Perhaps her Aunt Elizabeth would help her make sense of it all.

As she entered the house she spoke a greeting and was surprised at Elizabeth's response. Joyfully her elderly aunt cried out. "God has blessed you above all women, and your child is blessed! Why am I so honored that the mother of my Lord should visit me? When I heard your greeting, the baby in my womb leaped for joy. You are blessed because you believed that the Lord would do what He said!"

The two unlikely mothers hugged each other and laughed. Mary felt as if her heart might explode with praise if she kept silent any longer. Nearly shouting she cried,

"Oh, how my soul praises the Lord! How my spirit rejoices in God my Savior! For He took notice of His lowly servant girl and from now on all generations will call me blessed! For the Mighty One is holy, and He has done great things for me. He shows mercy from generation to generation to all who fear Him. His mighty arm has done tremendous things! He has scattered the proud and haughty ones. He has brought down princes from their thrones and exalted the humble. He has filled the hungry with good things and sent the rich away with empty hands. He has helped His servant Israel and remembered to be merciful. For He made this promise to our ancestors, to Abraham and his children forever!"

Together the women cried tears of joy then laughed as Elizabeth placed Mary's hand over the baby who continued to jump for joy in her tummy.

Elizabeth asked her young relative as she led her to sit down. "How far along are you dear?"

Mary was glad to finally be able to talk about her heavenly visitor. "The angel came to me with the news only seven days ago. I traveled here right away since I knew you would understand. He said you are in your sixth month so I was hoping to stay with you until your son is born. Maybe I can be of some help to you. Plus my time of mourning my father's passing will be over. By then maybe Joseph will know if he wants to follow through with our marriage."

Elizabeth peered into Mary's eyes. "So you have told Joseph? Does he understand that you carry the very Son of God?"

Mary shook her head slowly. "He knows that the baby is not his since we have not yet been together as husband and wife. But I'm afraid he thinks there has been another. He was very sad when I told him the news. My heart aches to think he could consider me unfaithful. On the journey here I prayed that the Lord would comfort him. Only our heavenly Father can give Josey peace. I trust that with the miracle of bearing God's Son, He will provide everything needed, even a husband to care for us."

Elizabeth hugged her young "daughter" and held her tongue. If word got out of Mary's pregnancy, the girl could be in grave danger. The law specifically demanded that an adulterous woman should be stoned to death. Surely God had a plan.

Though Elizabeth spoke not a word of her fears, Mary knew the law very well. She comforted Elizabeth with the same comfort with which she assured herself.

"If we make the Lord our refuge, if we make the Most High our shelter, no evil will conquer; no plague will come near our home; for He will order His angels to protect us wherever we go!"

Tears slipped down the face of the Godly old woman. "Yes my beloved sister. You are blessed because you believe that the Lord will do what He says! That is a rare quality and likely the reason you have been chosen to bear the Savior!"

Chapter Thirteen

Joseph seemed to carry the weight of the whole world on his shoulders. Though broad, they slumped with sadness. Dutifully he finished the home he had so lovingly prepared for Mary. But he doubted she would ever live there. He wondered whether to speak to his father about the things Mary told him. Only a few days earlier Joseph had convinced him to talk to his mother about going ahead with the wedding. Now it was impossible. Not only had Mary left Nazareth, but she had also confessed to carrying a child.

His father's cheerful tone broke through Joseph's misery.

"Good news my son! I have spoken to your mother and all is ready! How would you feel about claiming your beautiful bride tomorrow at sundown? Is a day enough time to make yourself presentable to the girl of your dreams?"

His father Jacob seemed as excited as Joseph had been earlier.

He wondered what to say. He must be careful. Mary's honor and perhaps even her life depended on it. Though it was hard to admit, Joseph still loved her very much.

"I'm sorry father. Mary has gone to be with her Aunt Elizabeth for a few months… at least until the bereavement year for her father is finished. So no wedding feast tomorrow. But please thank mother for me."

Jacob realized his son avoided looking at him and even continued as if too busy to talk about the matter. Something was amiss. Perhaps his youngest had cold feet. Otherwise, why would he allow Mary to make such a journey so close to the wedding?

He put his arm about Joseph's shoulders and noticed his sadness. "Talk to me son. What's going on?"

Joseph sighed. Surely his father could be trusted in such a delicate matter. Besides, the man had wisdom far beyond what Joseph could hope for. He looked into his father's eyes searching for help.

Recognizing the hesitation of the young man before him, Jacob encouraged his youngest to speak. "As iron sharpens iron, so one man sharpens another. Speak my son. Whatever is on your mind, I assure you I have been there before."

Joseph managed a laugh then a deep sigh.

"It's Mary. She said an angel visited her."

Jacob was surprised. "Well… you were right to laugh. I have never seen an angel. In fact, God has been silent for over four hundred years. But if Mary says she's been visited by a heavenly being, I would trust the girl. There is no one in Nazareth as virtuous as Mary."

Joseph sat down and his father sat beside him. He wondered whether to continue. The matter must be settled. At least his father knew enough of Mary to believe her word. He hated to cast doubt on the woman he loved.

Jacob urged his son to continue. "What did the angel reveal?"

Joseph remained silent as his father patiently waited.

Finally Joseph said the words. "Mary says she is to bear the Messiah. Apparently she is with child… but it is not mine. I have not been with her." He looked at his father. "I don't know what to do."

Jacob couldn't believe what he was hearing. Of all the women in

Nazareth Mary was the least likely to give herself to another. Jacob had been thrilled when his son chose her for his bride. Now this?

He paced the floor and stroked his beard. Suddenly he became angry and his words were frightening.

"Joseph! What if she has been assaulted? She lives alone in the poorest part of Nazareth! What if someone hurt her and no one heard her cry for help? She is a beautiful girl and I know that more than one man has had his eye on her. That's why I kept urging you to act quickly! The poor girl probably left home so she could feel safe until you make her your wife."

Joseph had wondered the same. But why wouldn't Mary tell him? Instead she had made up a tale about bearing God's Son and not fulfilling her role as Joseph's wife in order to remain "pure." None of it made sense… unless someone powerful had taken advantage of her and threatened the safety of her loved ones.

"Simon!" Jacob suddenly uttered the name under his breath. "Heli told me the man proposed to Mary before you did yet she turned him away. He must have been so angry! Plus he has the power and resources to get anything he wants without answering to the law!"

Joseph thought on his father's explanation and it suddenly made more sense to him than anything else he could think of. But there was still the problem of what to do.

Once Jacob calmed down a bit, Joseph spoke.

"But father, I love her. No one has to know that the child is not mine. I could travel to Judea, bring her home, and no one would be the wiser."

Jacob thought on his son's words and eventually offered his advice.

"But you will know Joseph. I think that if she continues to repeat the angel story you should give her a bill of divorcement. I know you care for her but you must be sure you can trust her to be truthful… and faithful. God's law demands it."

Joseph put his head in his hands as he realized his father's words were wise.

Chapter Fourteen

Old Zechariah shuffled about the house as if nervously awaiting someone's arrival. Elizabeth and Mary quietly smiled at the man's excitement. Eventually he walked outside.

"He hasn't spoken since he saw the angel in the temple. Apparently God's messenger struck him silent because of his unbelief. But he writes notes continually. The anticipation of having a son has brought such joy to our home. Our prayers so long ago have finally been answered!"

Mary smiled at the precious old woman who could no longer hide her growing midsection. Together they sewed clothes for the boys they would have. Elizabeth's time was growing near while Mary was still dealing with morning sickness.

"Our son is to be named John. No one in either of our families has that name, but that is what the angel Gabriel said to call him."

Mary looked up from her work. "The angel's name was Gabriel? That is the same angel the Lord sent to the prophet Daniel. I wonder if the angel who came to me was Gabriel."

Elizabeth smiled. "You my daughter certainly know the Scriptures well. The first day you arrived you greeted me with beautiful words of life from our Lord. No wonder you are to bear the Messiah. He will certainly grow up in a home where the Word of His Father is taught!"

"Thanks to my beloved parents! Oh how often they repeated the glorious truths. I have dreamed of doing the same for my own children. Now sweet Jesus, my firstborn, will get to hear the Words of His Father from my own lips and know they have forever changed my life."

"So your little one will be named Jesus? How fitting! I'm sure you know it means "God with us." Did you pick His name yourself?"

Mary shook her head. "The angel revealed it to me. I wonder what Josey is thinking about all this. I guess I'll know soon enough." She busied herself with her work and tried to think on the things she knew to be true. Joseph was good and would never do anything to hurt her. But more importantly, the Almighty was good too and had promised to be her shield and protection. Even if her only job was to bring the Savior into the world, that would be enough. What an honor! Happily she could join her Abba and Ima without regrets.

Elizabeth placed her gnarled hand upon that of the precious girl beside her.

"It's time dear Mary. Send Zechariah for the mid-wife. Or better still, go yourself. By the time he gets there I will have birthed this baby without her."

Mary laughed, hugged her aunt and rushed from the house. In the courtyard Zechariah paced and prayed. Apparently the old man had sensed the time was near. Mary motioned him inside and hurried away.

Chapter Fifteen

The months without Mary seemed like a lifetime. Joseph still didn't know what to do. She would be home soon and then what? He dreaded the conversation they must have and rehearsed it often in his head. No matter the outcome, he could not consider shaming her publicly. A private bill of divorcement would be the best option. He tossed on his bed as he thought of her. Their new home was perfect with plenty of hand-crafted furniture fashioned with her in mind. It only made him sadder.

He fell into a fitful sleep while asking the Almighty for direction.

As clear as day, an angel appeared to him with the answer.

"Joseph, son of David, do not be afraid to take Mary as your wife. For the Child within her was conceived by the Holy Spirit. She will have a Son, and you are to name Him Jesus, for He will save His people from their sins."

He sat straight up and looked around the room. The angel was no longer there. It mattered not as the message was clear. An old familiar passage from the book of Isaiah came to him as he considered the dream.

"Look! The virgin will conceive a Child! She will give birth to a Son, and they will call Him Immanuel, which means 'God is with us.'"

It had been right in front of him. The virgin the prophet spoke of was his own Mary! This virtuous woman had not been untruthful or promiscuous or any of the other things he had so foolishly considered. Sweet Mary was chosen by the Lord God Almighty! Just as she said, the Baby's name would be Jesus!

Joseph shook his head as the reality of his role sank in. He was to be the assumed father of God's own Son. Together they would raise this Boy who would, as the angel said, "Save His people from their sins!"

"Hallelujah!" he shouted then covered his mouth. He'd wake the whole family if he didn't contain himself. The walls were not that thick!

Quickly he dressed and thought of his next step. He must get to Mary and tell her of the angel's visit. Suddenly he recalled the day she shared the same news with him. How sad she must have been when he didn't believe her! Now three months later she probably still wondered where Joseph stood even as the very Son of God grew within her. As he gathered his things he prayed for his beloved Mary. Soon they would be together sharing the wonderful privilege assigned by God.

But first he must tell his father.

Chapter Sixteen

Jacob was less than thrilled when his son woke him. "It can wait until morning! Your mother and I have worried enough over the woman. Go back to bed before you wake the others!"

Joseph would not be quieted. He must leave immediately and wanted his father's blessing.

"Please father, I must tell you my news! A mighty angel appeared to me in a dream and I'm leaving to fetch Mary right away. Come so we can speak privately!"

Jacob sighed. "Oy! More angels! Enough already!"

His mother rolled over and lit the lantern. "Whatever you have to say can be said with me present. I know about your fiancée and the child she carries. You must put her away Joseph. She is not worthy of your devotion and I certainly don't want her living amongst us."

Joseph was deeply wounded. His mother's words and his father's sudden outburst surprised him.

"Quiet woman!" Jacob was angry that his wife spoke so callously. She would not be aware of the situation at all except that she had purposely eavesdropped. Then she had freely spoken the gossip to the other women of the house and nagged Jacob continually to push Joseph regarding the divorce.

Joseph tried again to defend Mary.

"Father, mother, please… I beg of you. God sent an angel tonight to direct me. I am to take Mary as my wife. She is the virgin spoken of by Isaiah who will bring the Messiah into the world. I have been chosen to protect them. And I need your blessing."

Jacob could tell his son would not be deterred so he rose from his bed. "Take whatever you need. Here. I have a little money tucked away. Use it wisely. But be very careful son. Wait until daybreak and find traveling companions. The road between here and Judea is filled with robbers. May the Lord be with you."

He hugged his son as he whispered.

"I am sorry that your mother will never believe the story you and Mary have… agreed upon. The wedding cannot be here. You would be wise to have Mary's uncle do the ceremony. Perhaps stay with them a while. Maybe that will answer some of the questions that will come later when it is apparent that the girl carries a child before marriage."

Joseph was crushed. His father's words revealed his doubt in Joseph's character. His mother's mournful sobs followed him as he left the family home without their blessing.

Chapter Seventeen

Elizabeth's strength was nearly gone. Mary held her hand and stroked her wrinkled brow. "You can do it Auntie! Stay strong! The mid-wife sees the head. One more big push and that son of yours will be making his presence known! Come on now... PUSH!!!"

Elizabeth bore down and pushed with all the energy she had left. She would deliver the boy or she would die trying!

Her scream fell on deaf ears but old Zechariah could tell by the looks on the faces of the crowd that had gathered. His wife was nearing the end. He fell to his knees and begged the Lord for mercy. This life-long companion had been his rock, his love, his thorn in the flesh, his best friend since they were wed so long ago. Together they had mourned the years without children. Then later they watched again as couples around them filled their homes with grandchildren. Often they had prayed that God would lift the curse that seemed to cover their home though they faithfully served Him year after year. Then finally they found themselves content with just each other. If he lost her now...

Silently the old man begged God for her life.

"Please dear God of mercies, let her live to enjoy the little one You so graciously have given us. He will be strong, a man of power and strength like Elijah as he prepares the way for the Messiah. Your angel told me that much. But Elizabeth! She is so frail. Please God... I beg of You... spare her life for me. I fear that I cannot go on without her."

A hand on his shoulder caused him to look up. Mary stood by his side weeping.

Yet she smiled.

She beckoned the old man into the room where his wife lay motionless. On her belly rested a healthy baby boy. But Elizabeth didn't move.

Zechariah knelt beside the wife of his youth and stroked her cheek. She opened her eyes and smiled. Her hand trembled as she reached for her husband.

"We did it old man!" Tears of joy mixed with exhaustion streamed down her face. To Zechariah, she had never looked more beautiful. She cried as she whispered,

"Bless the Lord, O my soul, and all that is within me, praise His sweet holy Name!"

Zechariah kissed her hand and silently praised God for sparing her life. Carefully he lifted his son and rested his tiny head on his shoulder. The old man wanted to shout the praise and joy that welled up within him but his voice would not come. Instead he cried tears of thanksgiving over the baby he held in his arms.

Mary too was exhausted. She walked outside and down the hill to her favorite grove of trees. Olive blossoms floated on the warm gentle wind. Alone there she knelt and cried out to God. She missed Joseph and wondered if he still cared. Reclining in the soft grass she felt herself drifting.

Peace washed over her soul as she realized. If God could perform such a miracle in Zechariah and Elizabeth's life, He would surely see Mary through the days ahead... with or without Joseph.

For as the angel had said, "Nothing is impossible with God!"

Chapter Eighteen

Joseph milled about town hoping to find other travelers so as not to go alone. His patience was spent. He was about to strike out on his own when a band of men approached. By the looks of things they were sojourners too. After a few inquiries which revealed they were on their way to Jerusalem to visit the temple he decided they'd make good traveling companions.

Each evening they set up camp before dark and shared food. He was glad for the bread his mother had baked ahead of time. Perhaps he would be able to appease her at some point once he and Mary got settled into married life. He knew most of his mother's anxiety was about how things would appear to their friends and neighbors. Joseph wondered if eventually the Son of God would be able to win his mother over. He smiled at the thought. The woman had always been a pushover for little boys.

After days of traveling the group arrived in Jerusalem. Though Joseph had been there many times he was still in awe of the temple. But his heart was with Mary in the Judean hillside. Though his companions urged him to stay, he was determined to finish his journey. Just as they were parting ways he spotted a group of folks headed toward the temple. Had his eyes deceived him?

It was her!

He broke into a run toward the group then stopped before he made a fool of himself on a public street. Her smile was his reward as she too nearly hugged him for joy. "Josey! You're here! What brings you to Jerusalem?"

He bowed but never took his eyes off her. "Why you dear Mary! I was hoping to see you!"

Though she laughed, tears sprang to her eyes. Joseph had not abandoned her.

"Come! We are going to the temple for the circumcision of Zechariah and Elizabeth's baby boy. Just look at their handsome son!" Old Zechariah beamed as Elizabeth presented the child.

"Wow! He's quite an armload! Look at all that hair! Next year at this time he'll have a beard like his papa!"

The group laughed at Joseph's words then made their way inside.

Mary gazed at her fiancé and thought about what a wonderful father he would make. No wonder God had chosen him to be her husband!

Chapter Nineteen

As the group of neighbors and friends entered the temple Mary lingered to talk with Joseph. "I'm so thankful the Lord allowed you to witness this wonderful day! The angel Gabriel appeared to Zechariah to let him know that he would have a son. This little boy will grow up to be like Elijah and prepare the way for the Messiah! Uncle Zechariah has been unable to speak since the angel appeared. But look at him! He is so happy! And Aunt Elizabeth is more alive than ever. As the angel said to me, "Nothing is impossible with God!"

Joseph smiled and whispered. "The Lord sent an angel to me too. He said we are to name His Son Jesus, just like you said!" Joseph bent low to speak so only Mary could hear. "I'm sorry I didn't receive your news at first. God knows I am a stubborn and stiff-necked man. How could I not believe you dear woman? Can you forgive me?"

Mary's heart beat fast at the nearness of Joseph as he whispered. Softly she replied.

"Yes my love. I have been praying for you night and day!"

Voices came from the crowd near Zechariah and Elizabeth. There seemed to be a dispute about something. Mary hoped her relatives would not allow anything to spoil their beautiful day.

"But there's no one in all of your family named John. He should be called Zechariah after his father!"

Elizabeth gave the order in no uncertain terms. "His name is JOHN!"

Certain ones in the crowd gestured to Zechariah regarding the child's name. They couldn't believe these faithful servants of God would break tradition and name the child such a common name. Obviously the boy was born to greatness. Zechariah motioned for a writing tablet and to everyone's surprise [except Elizabeth's] he wrote, "His name is John." Instantly Zechariah could speak and he began praising God. Filled with the Holy Spirit he prophesied in a strong voice.

"Praise the Lord, the God of Israel because He has visited and redeemed His people.

He has sent us a mighty Savior from the royal line of his servant David, just as he promised through His holy prophets long ago.

Now we will be saved from our enemies and from all who hate us.

He has been merciful to our ancestors by remembering His sacred covenant-

The covenant He swore with an oath to our ancestor Abraham.

We have been rescued from our enemies so we can serve God without fear, in holiness and righteousness for as long as we live.

And you, my little son, will be called the prophet of the Most High, because you will prepare the way for the Lord.

You will tell His people how to find salvation through forgiveness of their sins.

Because of God's tender mercy, the morning light from heaven is about to break upon us, to give light to those who sit in darkness and in the shadow of death, and to guide us to the path of peace."

Awe fell upon the whole crowd and the news spread throughout the Judean hills. Everyone who heard about it reflected on the events and asked, "What will this child turn out to be?" For the hand of the Lord was surely upon him in a special way.

As Mary pondered all these things she wondered if her day could get any happier. To her great surprise, it did.

Chapter Twenty

As the community of friends made their way back to Emmaus they seemed to speak softly to one another as if sharing a secret. Mary hardly noticed. She was just happy to have Joseph near. After a journey of several hours, Zechariah suggested they stop for rest under a nice tree. The other families hurried on as their children were still full of energy. Mary was certainly glad for the rest and wondered at the strength of her elderly relatives. She hoped since Joseph had arrived unexpectedly she wouldn't have to make her way back to Nazareth too soon. She still struggled with morning sickness, but more than that she hoped to help her aunt with the baby. Perhaps she could even learn things that would be helpful in days to come. As she silently pondered all of that, she noticed Joseph gazing at her. When he caught her eye he smiled mischievously.

Since it was only Zechariah's family there, Joseph felt he could freely speak. In fact he was more comfortable with them than he was his own family, especially since his mother had revealed her disdain for Mary.

He decided to ask again what he had asked the old man privately. In fact he made sure Mary heard this time.

"Father Zechariah, Mary and I have been betrothed for nearly a year and a half. If her groom were to come for her, say… tomorrow evening, would you be willing to perform the marriage ceremony?"

Mary caught her breath and covered her mouth with her hand. Tears sprang to her eyes as her Uncle Zechariah answered.

"It would be my most holy honor dear son! Elizabeth and I have been a part of many weddings. But none as important and special as this! Plus we just happen to have an upper room where Mary stays now that can serve as the bridal suite. You may stay as long as you'd like. Once again God has provided ahead of time what we didn't even know we needed!"

Elizabeth hugged Mary then pointed at Joseph with a crooked finger. "But for tonight, you will sleep in the courtyard!"

Elizabeth brought the garment from a sturdy cedar box and held it out to Mary. "This wedding gown is about a hundred years old, but it's yours if you want! I dreamed of passing it on to my daughter but it was not to be. Who knew our great God had a more wonderful plan. Now I can pass it on to you, the mother of the Son of God! Oh what a blessing my dear girl!"

Mary was overjoyed at the provision. Her own wedding garments were in Nazareth as she never dreamed Joseph would fetch her from her Uncle's home. At last her days of bereavement were over. She could adorn herself in the beautiful wedding clothes for Joseph as they promised their faithfulness to one another.

The days that followed were filled with both sadness and wonder. Together they returned to Nazareth. But instead of taking his bride to the home he had so lovingly prepared, they chose to live in Heli's old home. Gossip surrounded the couple especially since Joseph's parents did not host a marriage celebration. Mary hid her condition as long as she could, but a short six months later it was very evident. Though it was nearly time for her to deliver, Joseph felt it best to take her with him to the home of their ancestors. The government census could not be ignored. But surely some of the many relatives that lived in Bethlehem would welcome them there.

Chapter Twenty One

Again they were saddened. More family turned them away. To the local hostel they went, hoping beyond hope for a place to rest. The journey had been hard. Though Mary tried not to show it, she was in the beginning stages of labor. Deep breaths were no longer helping to relieve the pain. Four days of walking the rough countryside to Bethlehem were definitely taking their toll.

The concern on Joseph's face was evident. Even the innkeeper turned them away. But a small cave-like stable out back would give them a place to rest.

Mary watched as her husband pitched new hay then spread a blanket. Before she could make her way to the makeshift bed her water burst forth in a gush.

"Oh… Josey!" She held her back and cried out in pain as reality hit. There was no time to fetch a mid-wife. The man she had not been intimate with would soon deliver her son.

Quickly Joseph helped her lie down. Gently he spoke as he smoothed her brow. "I know how private you are dear woman. But this is going to happen. I can't risk leaving you to find help. But the Lord God Almighty is with us. HE will bring forth His Son!"

Mary let out an anguished cry and knew her husband spoke the truth. A few hours later, the bloody form of a healthy baby boy emerged. Quickly Joseph cleaned the child as best he could then passed him to his mother. Her arms trembled with exhaustion as she cuddled her infant son. Joseph washed then settled in beside her. Together they held each other and cried.

"I'm sorry I couldn't provide a better place for you Mary." Joseph reached for the boy as he apologized. "I was sure one of father's uncles would show hospitality."

Mary looked at her kind husband and silently thanked the Lord for him. "You did all you could. Now check the bag. I brought clothes for the baby."

Joseph reached with his empty hand into the travel bag and pulled out swaddling. Mary spread the cloth on her lap then wrapped the newborn tightly.

"Elizabeth showed me how." She smiled as she bundled her son. "That feeding trough will make a nice cradle for tonight. At least he can't fall out of that."

Joseph rose, emptied the manger, then added fresh straw.

Gazing at his wife holding her newborn, he whispered. "He's got your curls." Joseph shook his head in wonder. "Jesus! Sweet Son of God." He smiled.

Mary laughed. "Yes Jehovah saves! And with Him, nothing is impossible!"

Finale

A young man sat on the hillside of his family land. Once again, he was working third shift with a few others. Nothing had stirred the flock for months now, yet here he was, watching sheep. He wondered to himself if his father's words were true.

Gazing into the night sky, the verses played over in his head. His dad loved to quote Scripture.

"The faithful love of the LORD never ends! His mercies never cease. Great is His faithfulness; His mercies begin afresh each morning. I say to myself, 'The LORD is my inheritance; therefore, I will hope in Him!' The LORD is good to those who depend on Him, to those who search for Him. So it is good to wait quietly for salvation from the LORD. And it is good for people to submit at an early age to the yoke of His discipline."

He laughed a little. His dad always threw that last part in for good measure. Sure he was young, but it seemed like it was taking forever for him to really DO anything. Not only was he supposed to wait, but wait quietly, while he submitted to discipline. His dad liked to remind him often of the importance of being faithful in simple things. But shepherding is not all that noble. Would he ever be allowed to do anything really important?

Without warning, the darkness gave way to incredible radiant light. His heart felt as though it would melt in his chest. Never had he faced such fear. A voice came from the light, assuring him that all was well.

"I bring you good news of great joy to all people. The Savior- yes, the Messiah, the Lord- has been born today in Bethlehem, the city of David! And you will recognize Him by this sign: You will find the baby wrapped in swaddling clothes, lying in a manger."

Before he could question the wisdom of putting a baby in a feeding trough, the mighty angel that had spoken the words was surrounded! The skies were filled with a powerful army arrayed in light. Strength poured forth and thunderous voices shouted in unison,

"Glory to God! Glory to God in the Highest! Peace and good will toward men!!!"

He fell to his knees and realized he was worshiping with the heavenly host, very glad that the message was one of peace! Suddenly the visitors were gone. The night was dark once again. He rose on weak legs and moved toward his companions.

"Bethlehem is just across the way. Let's go!"

Normally he would worry about the flock. But his gut told him his father would be glad he left the sheep to see the child the angels spoke of.

"He's here!" shouted his friend.

He rounded the stalls and there, just as the angel had said, was a tiny baby. With the wrinkled face of a newborn, He stirred and gave a little cry. A tired mother rose to check on him. She lifted Him from the straw and said, "His Name is Jesus."

The young shepherd tentatively reached for the child as his mother smiled. A prayer of praise rose from the depths of his soul.

"Why dear God, would You choose a simple shepherd like me? Thank You Father, for putting me with the flock tonight! Salvation has come, and I hold Him in my arms! OH! Just wait until I tell my Abba!"

~~~*~~~

Purpose:

"But these are written so that you may believe that Jesus is the Messiah, the Son of God, and that by believing in Him you will have life by the power of His Name!" –John 20:31

I hope you enjoyed this fictional account of the birth of Christ. It's only fictional in the minor details which help to put flesh and bones on a story. And sometimes it's easier to share a story with a friend or relative than to open Scripture in the midst of a family gathering. So send it to whoever God puts on your heart. May the Lord bless the sharing of this story for His glory!

Resources:

Matthew Chapter one and two

Luke Chapter one and two

Psalm 23; 90; 91; 103

Lamentations 3:23

Jewish Betrothals and Weddings, Oasis Trade Links

Jewish Marriage Customs: Jewish marriage customs

The Jewish Wedding Analogy: Commentaries on Jewish Weddings

The Ancient Jewish Wedding: a Missing link in Christianity: Creation science-Jewish wedding-missing-link-Christianity

All these scripture references are from the NLT.

An Orange with Peppermint

By Roger Barbee

This morning my brother and I were talking on the
telephone. Like siblings who live far apart, we shared news of work,
children, grandchildren, sisters, and our mother. However, it was
when he began telling me about buying a box of oranges for a fund
raiser of one of his grandchildren that a memory came into focus.
And, like so many memories, this one had lain dormant for many
years in my mind, but when my brother began talking about
peppermint sticks and oranges, it and more of those Christmases in
Shadybrook came to life. In a world of technology, social media, and
limitless gadgets that keep us, if we choose, in touch with the world,
those long-ago Christmases will seem strange because of what we
children wanted. We had little and expected little at Christmas, so any
gift, no matter how small, was great. And one of the gifts we came to
anticipate was fresh fruit, nuts, and some candy. That is where our
church played a major role.

All it was, was a number 2 brown paper bag given out the
Sunday before Christmas to all the children. In each bag the deacons
had dropped a mixture of nuts, an apple, an orange, and a
peppermint stick. The peppermint was red and white stripped, the
apple small, and the orange thin skinned. The nuts, except for the
pecans, were difficult for little fingers to open. However, we were
hungry, and this was food, especially the orange and peppermint
stick.

As I remember, there was an order to eating the contents of
those little, brown bags. Because of its condition, the often-bruised
apple, out and out mealy, was soft and somewhat brown, so it was
eaten right away. Next came the thin-skinned, small orange. Using
what we called a case-knife out of mother's kitchen, a pyramidal hole
was cut in the top and out of this hole all the juice was sucked until
the orange was limp. It was then that the peppermint stick was peeled
of its thin wrap and the straight end inserted into the orange. If you

52

were fortunate, the stick and orange treat would last for an entire morning or afternoon. Finally, when everything had been eaten but for the nuts, we would attack them with the handle of the case knife. Sometimes we could glean enough meat from one of the nuts to eat, but often the small hands and knife handle managed only to make a mess of shattered shells and pulp under the metal-topped kitchen table.

A Christmas like those we shared in Shadybrook seems almost foreign to me now. If my brother and I had not agreed on so much shared memory, I would doubt the accuracy of mine. Yet, our world then was so small and limited and poor that a brown bag with two fruits, some nuts, and one candy cane was something to anticipate. As I think about gift-giving today, I have to question it, and I wonder if more is more or is more less or is less more. I see what children are given today and while not resentful, I doubt its wisdom. The merchants of America have been selling us consumers "stuff" for Christmas presents since just after Halloween. We are told that more is better. We are offered deals. We are consumed with consuming. We enjoy giving and receiving stuff. But I doubt.

On this balmy afternoon two days before that birth, I reflect and have to wonder. I can't go back in time and re-live those early days of oranges and peppermint sticks. I can't change what was in order to see if I would have felt happier with more than those brown bags. But I can still feel the excitement of being given that simple gift at church and carrying it home as my mother walked with us along Bethpage Road. Inside our little house she had managed on her mill wages to have a Christmas tree fully decorated and each of us would have a present under it. Somehow. And we had our orange with peppermint, an apple, and those gosh-awful nuts.

Preparing our hearts for Christmas

By Doug Creamer

I don't know how you are doing on your Christmas list, but mine is getting down to the last couple of things to get done. The outside has looked like Christmas since Thanksgiving; the inside is slowly making progress. It's the same way with me. On the outside, I have been wearing all my Christmas ties, I look ready for Christmas. But on the inside, my heart is not quite ready for Christmas. I've been reading and reflecting on the Christmas story and I feel like my heart is moving in the right direction.

I've been thinking a lot about Mary the last couple of weeks. In my career I have taught a number of girls who had children. In many of the cases, the guy was nowhere to be found, leaving the girl with the responsibility of bringing the child into the world and raising it up all alone. It must be difficult, even in our society which is much more open to this type of situation.

When Mary agreed to be the mother of our Lord, she probably didn't realize all she would have to go through. She told the angel and God "yes" and that decision nearly cost her everything. The leaders in town decided that Mary needed to die because they assumed she had been unfaithful to Joseph. Even Joseph had decided to break off the engagement because he didn't understand. She was scorned and ridiculed.

I imagine that Mary felt scared, alone, and maybe even abandoned by God as the people she knew attacked her good name. I wonder if Mary wished she could change her mind after she saw the way she was treated. Even Joseph doubted her story; I mean honestly, would you believe it? The path is often not easy for those who dare to say yes to God.

We honor Mary now, but I bet it was difficult to make the journey to Bethlehem. They didn't understand why they had to go to Bethlehem at that specific time, but God was working to fulfill His word. The moment arrives for the birth of the baby and there she is in a dark and smelly cave. In all probability Mary didn't have her family and close friends nearby to help her. They were poor, in a strange place, and unprepared to be the parents of God's only son.

They were much like you and me, unsure of what to do next. They must have decided to settle in Bethlehem because they were still there two years later when the wise men arrived. God's plan called for them to move to Egypt before moving back to Nazareth. Do you know what is amazing? God knew everything before it all happened. He prepared the way and I believe he was waiting for them when they arrived. He met their needs but they still had to struggle to find their way. He sent His angels to guide and protect them, but they still had to obediently follow where He was leading them.

Jesus arrived humbly in a manger so every human being could approach Him. He understood royalty yet lived in meager circumstances. He endured everything we do from pain, suffering, rejection, anger, temptation, humiliation, and the list goes on, so He could understand our circumstances. He's lived through tough times, so He can relate to us when times are tough. Jesus came as God's messenger of love to the world because God loves each person and wants a relationship with them.

Christmas is God's message of love to a world that desperately needs His guidance. God's gifts of love, peace, and joy are for all mankind. The message of Christmas offers hope in the direst of circumstances. Jesus offers salvation, deliverance, freedom, and unimaginable joy.

Jesus is knocking on the door of your heart. I encourage you to open your heart to Him. He wants to bring peace of heart, mind, and soul to you. He wants to restore your joy. For those who feel lost, He has come to show you the path to life. As Mary learned, it's not an easy path, but one thing you can be sure of: He will never leave or forsake you. So turn your life and all your circumstances over to baby lying in a manger, who died for your sins, and who is resurrected and waiting for your arrival in Heaven. Merry Christmas, and God bless us, every one!

Behind the Christmas Door

By David Freeze

I shared a bedroom with my brother growing up. Our bed faced the door to the house's living room. On most days, this wasn't a big deal and we didn't use that door much. The living room was more or less off limits unless we had company coming or one of us had to practice the piano. But the Christmas season always made this room the center of our small home.

Usually the room wasn't even heated regularly. I didn't think much of it at the time, but this practice had something to do with the door almost always being closed. Near the holidays, the room was more likely heated and sometimes the door was left open. Still, from bed, I usually looked at the closed door as nothing special.

Why was that door, a solid pine one painted white, so special only during the Christmas season? In the last few days ahead of Christmas, anyone who visited ended up in that room and the conversation continued around the tree, other decorations and any gifts that might already be there. Some of the gifts were for friends and other family members, waiting for the perfect time to share them. Should any of those gifts be meant for the particular group of visitors, an exchange was likely in order. And only rarely could we open any other gifts on hand ahead of Christmas Day.

As the remaining days until Christmas melted away, the pattern was inconsistent. Sometimes the door was open, sometimes not. But finally as we went to bed on Christmas eve, the door was closed securely. And I knew as a small boy, that many special and even magical things would happen on the other side of the door overnight.

I had just a small part in the preparation for any possible special happenings on the door's other side. My only job as I remember was to leave Santa a few tree shaped Christmas sugar cookies and a glass of fresh milk, recently brought to the house from our own dairy.

Once in bed, I began to wonder if I could hear anything during the night through that door. I remembered what it looked like on the other side and imagined Santa arriving to place his gifts just so. Would he take time to eat my cookies and drink some milk, or would he even see them? Late in the night, I remember listening and hoping for any sound. I strained to see if a light came on, even something as small as a candle, that might illuminate the door frame.

I had no thoughts of needing to sleep! Nothing important could be missed and I had to be alert just in case. In the dark, the door seemed even a little bit foreboding. If I heard a noise, would I even have the courage to open the door and meet Santa face to face? I would face that dilemma if I just heard a noise or saw any type of light, not wanting to miss Santa in my own house. No concept of time entered my head. I wanted very early morning to come, ready to see the other side of that door.

All of this or some version kept me alert, until I fell asleep, which happened every year. Try as I might, not once could I stay awake through the night. My sister slept in the other end of the house and my brother slept the night in the same bed where I was. Neither had the same intent as me, an intense desire to miss nothing.

Eventually the time came! I can't remember a clock in the room as a small boy, and don't exactly know how the time seemed right. It was up to me to get up and open that door, when I simply couldn't wait any longer. I more than expected that Santa would have come and gone and felt confident that he would have answered my letter. Gifts for the family that I requested would be there and yet another Christmas day would begin. As soon as I opened the door…..

Not Buyin' It

By Lynna Clark

As I shopped for jeans for my beloved, I noticed this ad in the men's department, with a caption that says, **"The perfect gifts for everyone…"**

Are you kidding me? Mister ruggedly handsome wades deftly to shore while sporting his new man purse. His shirt, and sweater, are all **tucked into his khakis**. Who fishes like that?

What man is going to look at that picture and think**, "Oh goody!** I DO hope I get that for Christmas! What a perfect gift!"
I see that picture and wonder why he's out wading in his church clothes. What's in that man purse anyway… a hairbrush and a mirror? I hope he brought a sandwich because I sure don't see any evidence on his ensemble that he'll be frying fish.

Of course we all know that if we gave our husbands such an outfit the first thing we'd say after he opened it would be **"FISH SLIME AND BAIT GUTS ARE HARD TO GET OUT OF A SWEATER! <ins>DO NOT WIPE YOUR HANDS ON YOUR NEW CLOTHES!</ins>"**

Maybe that's why he carries a man purse

… for his wet-wipes

… and possibly some earplugs if he lives with a woman like me.

Sorry.

I just read back over this and it sounds pretty harsh.

My apologies to the pretty man… bless his heart.

I guess everyone has to make a living.

Besides, a poster with a man dressed like Larry the Cable Guy probably wouldn't sell that many sweaters.

… or man purses.

Perhaps that's why Larry endorses reflux medication.

Now THAT makes sense.

Sweet Savor

By Ann Farabee

Our five senses seem more alive during the holiday season, don't they?
Christmas is special enough that it can touch all five senses at once.

The sounds of Christmas - music, laughter, the ringing of bells.
The sights of Christmas - decorations, lights, families gathering.
The tastes of Christmas - food, food, and more food.
The joys of touch at Christmas - hugs, gifts, something touching our heart.
The smells of Christmas - the tree, the baking, the candles.

Genesis 8:20 says that Noah built an altar to the Lord.
Genesis 8:21 says that the Lord smelled a sweet savor.

It is amazing to think of God smelling a sweet savor.
Close your eyes and envision that for a second.
The Lord smelling a sweet savor when we use our altar of prayer.
The thought of that may make us want to pray more often.

We should take time to pray.
We should go to our altar.
Surrender.
Cry out to God.
As the Lord hears our prayer, the sweet savor will begin to fill the air.

Where is our altar?
-In our heart.
-In our home.

-In our house of worship.

During this holiday season, let's build our altar.
Let's use our altar.
And…may it be a sweet savor to our Savior.

Lord, help us to build our altar. Help us to use it. May it be a sweet savor to You. Amen

Merry Christmas to Me!

By Lynna Clark

Nothing says Happy Holidays better than a concealed carry class. So we signed up for one being offered the Saturday after Thanksgiving. We sat in a class from nine a.m. to nearly six p.m. So much information had to be covered that the instructor gave the wonderful option of only taking a twenty minute lunch break. Guys took off to the nearest gas station for pizza and wings and such. We opted to stay put and eat our granola bars. Okay, so there might have been a Snicker consumed as well. I am not myself when I'm hungry. Everyone seemed very knowledgeable; especially the man sitting beside me who travels for a living and happens to know every gun law in every state. Silently I begged God to muzzle the dude so that we could just be done. I on the other hand, tried to disappear and hoped not to be called upon. I wondered what in the world had possessed me to take the class.

I fully expected to be brought to the front after the instructor graded my paper. I imagined a scene where he offered. "The bad news is you failed. The good news is that you can go get supper now."

At that point I hardly cared. I was shaking hungry. After taking the written exam we would proceed to the shooting range. He warned us about the computer screen at each shooting booth. "Only hit the buttons I tell you or you'll jack the whole system up." Another terrible scene flashed through my very tired brain. I was confident in one thing. If anyone was going to hit the wrong button, it would be me.

Eventually it was my turn to shoot. When I stepped into my booth the screen went blank. I was not about to touch that thing. Our instructor came over and brought the choices up on the screen. Quickly he told me how to move the target. With ear protection on I couldn't hear what he was saying. Plus every shot the other students took made me jump like a cricket in a chicken coop. I was so nervous and so hungry I could hardly steady the gun. Several deep cleansing breaths later, I settled in and began shooting. Even as nervous as I was, all I had to do was imagine someone trying to snatch one of my grandchildren. The poor target guy never stood a chance.

It was time to move the target farther away. In order to pass the class I would have to fire thirty rounds into what would be considered center mass... in other words, more bad guys snatching sweet grandbabies. But this time they'd be across the yard.

A hot flash came like molten lava and hit my own center mass. It was so intense it fogged up my protective eyewear. Seriously. I couldn't see a thing. My hands were shaking and my heart was pounding.

But guess what.

I did it.

With a little swagger, I turned in the noise reducing headgear, the sweaty eyewear and my target with all but three holes in the middle of a very bad man. On the way home we drove through Chick-fil-a where it was their pleasure to toss food into a bag. It might've been the best meal I've ever had. I dripped Polynesian sauce down the front of my best shooting shirt but it didn't even matter.

Jingle bells and shotgun shells! I did it!

Merry Christmas to me!

The Christmas Letter

By Roger Barbee

Call me a curmudgeon or even a Grinch, but I despise those Christmas letters. You know the ones I mean—the egoistical ramblings that attempt to tell you all that has happened to its family since the letter last Christmas. They give me news that I am either not interested in or that I already know, such as the big wedding that took place last summer. It seems to me that if a family and I have a relationship, then I am aware of the important events of the last year. Yet, here they come in droves with the accompanying photograph of them all smiling with no signature or hand-written message. However, this week I received a different kind of Christmas letter.

This letter, like most Christmas letters, is a typed page. It informs about the writer and his family, and some of what is written I knew. Yet, this letter is different because the writer has made his letter personal by sharing his family's life this past year, not listing a litany of facts and events that seems to go on forever and is always happy. His letter is honest, not phony. His letter shares, it does not tell. His letter shows the bones of his-and his children's-life this past year, it does not gloss over. His letter is a tribute to living right, not a glorification of earthly accomplishments. It is a letter of thanksgiving, not getting.

In his letter he shares how he and his six children placed his wife and their mother in an assisted living facility because she could no longer care for herself, and neither could he or the children. She recognizes family members, but she has "no emotion about anything." Each day he shares lunch with her. He writes how "Our Christian faith has sustained us through all of our 64 years of marriage," and "We have always been thankful for the Almighty, for the wonderment of our children and their spouses." There is sadness in his letter, but also joy. The joy written about in the Gospels, the joy that sustains a person. The joy of having a friend like Leo.

Christmas Love

By Doug Creamer

The magical moment has finally arrived. All the hype from advertisers will soon be over and we can enjoy the peaceful arrival of our Lord and Savior. Here in the South it seems we will enjoy a warm Christmas Day, but people in many other parts of the country are stuck in winter's icy grip. Whether cold or warm, I hope we will all enjoy the warmth of family and friends on this special day.

Christmas affords most of us the opportunity to spend time with loved ones, to catch up on the year gone by, and to dream about the coming opportunities that the New Year holds. It is intended to be a time of love, joy, and peace. The reality for some is far from that as life has pushed them to their limits. The current economic situation, poor health, and a number of other variables have sought to steal the joy of the season.

It's difficult to believe in a God who loves you when you are going through difficult times. The irony is that is exactly what will sustain you through the tough and unbearable moments. God's love has the power to change our perspective on our situation, to give us the hope that we can overcome life's circumstance. God's love has the power to break through the darkest places of our lives and illuminate the path to freedom.

God's love is unselfish and He is deeply concerned for our lives. I believe there is a misconception about His love that is important to understand. Many people believe that they can act any way they want and God will still love them. God does love us, but there are consequences for disobedience. He is not a spineless God who allows us to do whatever we want, rather He expects us to walk in His ways.

Consider Jonah, who directly disobeyed God. He had to live in the belly of a large fish for several days. There were many kings who chose to worship false gods and they were removed from their thrones. Some may argue that those examples are from the Old Testament and that Jesus changed all that. Allow me to remind you of Ananias and Sapphira. They lost their lives for lying to God.

There are consequences for our sins and disobedience to God, but if we repent and turn back to God we will find Him waiting, in love, for us. It's like parents who try to teach their children something as simple as no. I don't know of anyone who wants to hear no, but it's important to help children understand this very simple concept. In my Christian walk God has said no to me and if I hadn't learned that lesson from my parents I would have been in deep spiritual trouble.

The Christ of Christmas comes with love in His heart, but its love that desires that we grow up into mature Christian adults. The Christ of Christmas wants us to discern right from wrong and make good choices. He wants us to fulfill the purpose for which we were created. He wants us to use the gifts that He has given us to make our world a better place in which to live. He wants us to share the love we have received from Him with those around us who are hurting, lonely, and in need of His affirming love.

I know that the love of God has changed my life. I am so glad that He came as a little child born in the most humble of circumstances so He could relate to me. He understands our human frailty and our weakness for sin. He's seen and experienced the trials of life. He was unjustly accused and condemned to death, yet even in that dark moment of His life, He still loved us. He came to die so we could experience God's love and have a relationship with Him. That's love.

If you have never received the greatest gift of God's love, I want to encourage you to open that package this Christmas. God's love, the love we find at Christmas, has the power to change your life, your circumstances, and your eternal destiny. I pray that you and your family have a special Christmas, whether you are together or apart, let God's love unite you. God demonstrated his perfect love in that little manger so many years ago. God bless you & Merry Christmas.

Give the Gift

By Ann Farabee

Our eyes met as I was rounding Aisle 7 of the grocery store. I knew her and wanted to talk with her because I had heard she was going through a very difficult time. But at the same time, it was almost Christmas and the holiday cooking had already begun. I was in a hurry and did not feel I had time to stop. But I did. And I was glad.

We hugged. We cried.
She talked. I listened.
We prayed together on Aisle 7.

As we went our separate ways, I said these words, "I will be praying for you."

I prayed for her the next day. And the next. And probably even the next.

But… one day I realized my promise to pray for her had been short-lived.

I blamed my memory. I blamed my busy life. I blamed everything - but myself.

I'll be praying for you. Important words that I meant were soon forgotten.

When I pray, God hears. God listens.
When I pray for someone, I am giving that person a gift.

It is called the power of prayer.
We have a direct link.
Luke 18:1 says we ought always to pray.

Do we believe it matters? Yes.
Do we believe God's Power is greater than our power? Yes.
Do we believe God hears our prayers? Yes.
Do we believe we pray enough? No.
Can we change that? Yes.
Will it be worth it? Yes.

Lord, help me to faithfully give the gift of prayer. Help me to remember to pray for someone when I say I will. Amen

The Star

By Ann Farabee

The wise men saw the star and went looking for the Savior. Something about that star was different.

They may have been astrologers. Maybe God sent a special star that night so they could find Jesus. It certainly would have been appropriate for such a time as this, since God's Son had come to save the world!

The star had their attention. Can you almost hear them exclaiming, "LOOK AT THAT STAR! CAN YOU BELIEVE IT?"

Enter King Herod. He was troubled by the news. He secretly called together the wise men to find out what time the star had appeared. He sent them to travel to Bethlehem to search for the young child that had been born, so that he could come worship him. But… his real plan was to have Jesus killed.

Using the star to navigate their way to Jesus was easy, because the star stood over where the young child was. When they saw it, they rejoiced with exceeding great joy.

When they saw Jesus, they fell on their faces and worshipped.

They then opened their treasures - the best they had to offer - gold, frankincense, myrrh. They presented them to Jesus.

The visit was complete. It was time to go home. But, somehow, life seemed different. They had been with Jesus. They would not be going back the same direction they had come, but would now go a different way - the direction God was leading them.

This story has been brought to you from Matthew 2:1-12.
No wonder we call them wise men.

Lord, may I be led by a star. May I look for the Savior. May I rejoice with great joy. May I see Jesus. May I fall down and worship. May I open my treasures. May I present them to You. May I go the direction You lead me. Amen

Heavenly Peace

By Ann Farabee

The tree goes up in our home every November 9th.
It comes down late on December 25th.

I sometimes consider myself a Scrooge when it comes to Christmas decorating.

I am not a super helper, but I am a super supervisor.

The ornaments are my favorite part, for they remind me of Christmas memories. I am sure the family enjoys me sharing memories of each ornament every year as it is placed on the tree.

Sadly, most of the year, ornaments are stored in the attic. Sometimes on their way to storage, they may get broken or separated from their ornament friends. At times, I have had to gently toss them into the trash when no one was looking.

As the decor was going up this year, I noticed a larger ornament that was a manger scene. It looked rough. The edges were jagged and it was starting to fall apart. Did I dare to toss it? No one was looking.

I began to look at it.
How could they not have made room at the inn?
The manger looked like a feeding trough in a cave?
The mother of the Savior of the World giving birth in a manger?
How must she have felt?

Did she have peace that night?

Yes. She had peace. She had accepted Jesus as her Prince of Peace.
No Jesus. No peace.
Know Jesus. Know peace.

The manger scene was definitely not tossed.

Lord, cover me with Your heavenly peace. May I remember that like Mary, I too, know the Prince of Peace. Amen

Holiday Adventure

By Ann Farabee

I sneaked out early, before the family woke up. I was going to beat the holiday crowd to a special store to get a special Christmas gift for a special child.

I got the best parking spot. That was a plus.
I wasn't wearing my pj's - but some may have thought I was.

In and out quickly. That was my plan.
Being inconspicuous was my goal.
But there she was at the door: THE GREETER.
She was glad to see me.

"Are you ready to get your holiday adventure started?" she asked.

I made eye contact, gave a 'half smile' and buried my head among some items for sale, as I whispered, "I'm just looking."

She cheerfully pointed out a couple of things she thought I would love, told me to enjoy my adventure, and to let her know if I needed her.

I hurriedly grabbed an item and walked to the other side of the store.
Shopping was not what I would refer to as a holiday adventure.

There she was. Greeter #2. Excitedly smiling, she said sweetly, "Good morning! Oh, I love what you picked out!"

I stopped. I glanced back toward Greeter #1 on the other side of the store. She waved. I then looked again at Greeter #2, who continued to beam with excitement.

I gave up. I smiled. I talked with them about the item I had found and why I thought the child I was giving it to would love it. Unintentionally, I had switched over to a good mood. It really was simple. It was more fun, too.

Against the wishes of my 'stony' heart that morning, I had given in and allowed myself to have a holiday adventure - not because of the stuff in my bag - but because of the greeters in the store.

I felt I left the store with more in my heart than I had in my shopping bag.
But - it is the most wonderful time of the year!
We may as well enjoy it.

Lord, may I enjoy the holiday season. May I not think of it as too busy, but instead may I see it as it is - a holy time. May I remember that You gave the greatest gift at Christmas - the gift of Your Son - Jesus Christ. Amen

Two Shirts and Food

By Ann Farabee

My husband and I had a 6 month old son and a 3 year old daughter. We had no way to pay our bills that month. We definitely had no way to buy our Christmas gifts.

But God showed up.
Our pastor called to tell us that the church would be providing our Christmas for us.

They paid our bills for December.
They brought us a Christmas tree.
They brought a Christmas Eve meal.
They brought a Christmas morning breakfast.
They brought gifts for our family.

When I remember that day, I mostly remember our living room. It was covered with gifts for my two little ones - who would have had none. And there was a gift for me - the most beautiful coat I had ever seen.

Has anyone ever asked you about your favorite Christmas?
I just told you about mine. It was amazing.

Luke 3:11 (NIV) John answered, "Anyone who has two shirts should share with the one who has none, and anyone who has food should do the same."

Lord, we thank You that we have two shirts and that we have food. Help us to remember to help others. Amen

Puzzled

By Ann Farabee

At our house, the Christmas holidays always involve working a puzzle of 1000 pieces.

There are many puzzle working strategies.

These are some of our favorites:

*Let the picture on top of the box be your guide.
*Find a good workspace.
*Open the box.
*Sort the pieces as needed.
*Build the framework first.
*Make connections. Connect your connections with other connections.
*Keep looking back at the top of the box.

Soon, your puzzle will be complete and wonderfully made!

Hmm? Perhaps these strategies could work in our daily lives.

*The top of the box would be our guide - God's Word.
*Find a workspace. That way, we will be at the place where God can use us.
*Open the box. Until we open the box, we will not receive what is inside.
*Sort. It will help us keep the main thing the main thing.
*Build the framework. It will provide strength and support.
*Make connections. Connecting is one of the most important things we do.
*Never lose sight of the top of the box. You will need it. That is where we can make sense of it all and let the pieces of our lives come together to serve His purpose.

Colossians 2:10 says we are complete in Christ.
Psalm 139:14 says that we are wonderfully made.

Lord, in times that we are puzzled by life, help us remember that You are our framework and that we are complete and wonderfully made. Amen

Shopping

By Ann Farabee

The wise men brought gifts to baby Jesus. They were gold, frankincense, and myrrh.

If the wise men went shopping, so should we.

Thanksgiving Day - 3pm. Stores were opening. The shopping season had begun. I refused to believe that Black Friday had the best deals.

Not me. I opted for shopping from home on Thanksgiving Thursday. A cup of coffee, a slice of pecan pie, and my computer. I smiled as I saw that everything was 40% off! I knew it! Shopping with the crowd on Black Friday had no real advantage!

I shopped. I did it! $600 worth for only $360. I proudly shut down my computer - and rewarded myself with a turkey sandwich. I was a super shopper!

Friday morning arrived. An email informed me that everything was now 50% off. Mental math informed me that my $600 purchase could have been $300 - not the $360 I had spent. It was heartbreaking.

Too much time had been spent looking for what I thought was the best deal - and it ended up not being the best deal.

However, there is one great deal none of us can afford to pass up! Here is the info:

DEAL OF THE DAY! IT'S FREE! You do not even have to make the purchase! Jesus died on the cross for our sins to purchase our salvation!

Don't know how to locate the deal?
Here is the special access code: John 3:16

For God so loved the world that He gave his only begotten Son, that whosoever believes in Him should not perish, but have everlasting life.

As for Black Friday? And the greatest Door Buster?

No sale - or gift of any price - could begin to compare with the gift the world was given on the darkest Black Friday - as Jesus gave His life for our sins.

And three days later, He became the real Door Buster - as He burst forth from the tomb - giving the world the greatest gift ever given - victory over death!

It was - and is - the deal of a lifetime!

Lord, help us to never become complacent about the gift of a lifetime that You freely gave to all who will accept it. Amen

Master Builder

By Ann Farabee

At my home, we have an abundance of Legos. Christmas always means more will be coming - that is if there are some available that we do not yet own.

Here are some of the Legos in our collection:

Taj Mahal, Roller Coaster, Ferris Wheel, Treehouse, Empire State Building, Parisian Restaurant, Bank, Detective's Office, Statue of Liberty, Wind Turbine, US Capitol Building, Ship in a Bottle, Great Wall of China, International Space Station

That equals a grand total of 30,445 Legos.

What if we took all those Lego structures apart and put them in one big pile?

Can you imagine that?

Each Lego piece was added to the structure one piece at a time.
Each Lego structure had a foundation.
Each Lego structure had a framework.

If we looked through the 30,445 Lego pieces, none of them would really be considered to be a superstar piece. But each Lego piece was important and had a role to fulfill - a place that it needed to be in order for the structure to be perfect and complete. None of the Lego pieces were as special apart as they would be in the place they were meant to be.

1 Corinthians 3:9-10 says that by God's grace, we are wise master builders. We are building our lives. We should build them carefully. We can do that by doing the right thing, making the right choices, and allowing Jesus to be the foundation of it all.

Lord, help me to be a wise master builder while allowing You to be the foundation of it all. Amen

Christmas Morning

By Ann Farabee

When I was growing up, Christmas was very special. My parents went above and beyond! Christmas food was plentiful for at least a week. Christmas gifts seemed to be much more than we deserved and maybe more than my textile mill working parents could afford.

On Christmas Eve, as I lay in bed in the room I shared with my siblings, I would listen for sounds of Santa in the living room. Apparently, he always arrived right after I fell asleep.

After a long restless night for me, my dad would come to our room and say, "Looks like somebody's been here!" That meant we could get up and see what was waiting for us!

Our living room would be overflowing with gifts. We spent our entire day looking through them, trying them on, using them, or playing with them. Late in the evening, we would try to find the perfect spot to keep the gifts that were now a part of our home.

Christmas night would come and the day was over. But, I was still happy, even though the gifts had been opened and put away. I was still happy, even though the tree had been put back in the box. I was still happy, even though the decorations were gone.

The star on top of the tree would be the last memory of Christmas to be put away. It was a gold star with a white light behind it. It was beautiful, and I always handled it carefully, so we could use it again next year.

I still think of that star. Just looking at it seemed to tell a story of hope - just like it did that night at the manger when the Light of the World was born.

Just like it did when the wise men saw his star and came to worship him.

Just like the gold star with the white light that I take out of its box year after year and place on my family's Christmas tree - still does.

I love that Christmas is still special - no matter our age.

Lord, thank You for the story of hope that we have because of Jesus. Amen

Love

By Ann Farabee

We wish you a Merry Christmas!
We wish you a Merry Christmas!
We wish you a Merry Christmas!
And a Happy New Year!

What is a wish? It can be defined as a desire, longing, or hope for something. It may not be easily attainable.

So, that could mean that a WISH may take some WORK to bring about.
And working to bring about the wish could make our Christmas more merry!

Perhaps the greatest Christmas wish would be a wish for love.
A wish for love can be a wish to receive love - or a wish to give love.

1 Corinthians 13 reminds us of some truths about love:
* Love is patient.
* Love is kind.
* Love does not envy.
* Love does not lift itself up.
* Love is not proud.
* Love does not easily provoke.
* Love thinks no evil.
* Love rejoices in truth.
* Love bears all things.
* Love believes all things.
* Love hopes all things.
* Love endures all things.

Love never fails. Love shows we care.
Love is the greatest attribute we can have - because God is love.

This wish of love WILL take some work, as we strive to love others as God loves us.

For God SO LOVED the world that He GAVE His only son. Not only did He love the world - He SO LOVED the world.

Lord, may this Christmas be a season where I remember how much I love. May I show love. Help me to love as You love. Amen

Seek Him

By Ann Farabee

There is something special about a Christmas tree decorated by family and placed in a dominant place in our homes. It somehow changes the atmosphere. As long as I can remember, I have loved to slip away into the room where the tree is, so I can stare at it for a few minutes. It sparks joy in my heart.

As a teacher, I have always liked a tree with a variety of ornaments, mostly because I have saved the ornaments given as gifts from my students. By the way, according to my ornaments, I am the World's Best Teacher!

I have been given ornaments from family and friends that each year take me on a trip down memory lane, as I fondly reminisce about special times and special people in my life.

The ornament that stands out the most to me is larger than the others, and it has five words on it that grab my attention every time I see it on the tree.

The words are: WISE MEN STILL SEEK HIM

There is great truth in those words.
We are wise if we seek Him.

Where can He be found?
Anywhere. Everywhere. In our hearts. In our heads.
While looking at a Christmas tree.

Matthew 2:1-2 says that the wise men had seen the star in the east and had come to worship Him.

They had been looking for Jesus!
They found Him!
They worshipped Him!

Lord, help me be wise and seek You. Amen

Count it all Joy

By Ann Farabee

Tis the season to be jolly. Fa la la la la la la la la. Most certainly, if you know this song, you sang it in your head as you read the words.

Not only do we have a holiday season in which we can be jolly - but we also have a reason to be jolly. Isaiah 9:6 says, "For unto us a child is born, unto us a son is given." (KJV) Jesus, the Savior of the World was born - and that is the reason for the season!

The holiday season is a busy season, but it is also a blessed season.

Busy can mean having a great deal to do. Blessed can mean holy.

Christmas is centered around the celebration of the birth of Jesus, which is the greatest event in the history of the world. No wonder it has become so busy - and so blessed.

To be jolly - and to have joy - can both mean to be happy.
Is there a season in which we should be jolly and have joy?
Yes. They all are.

James 1:2 says for us to count it ALL joy, even when we fall into trials. (KJV)

Having joy and being jolly - it's not just a good idea.
It's a God idea.

Lord, may I have joy and be jolly during this holiday season. Help me not to feel stress because of the busy schedule, but to feel blessed because of the reason for the season - the birth of my Lord and Savior, Jesus Christ. Amen

Stay Awake

By Ann Farabee

The news was everywhere! The college football National Championship had been decided by a game winning pass with one second remaining and the team I was pulling for had won. My first thought as I saw the news when I awoke was, "If I had known that was going to happen, I would have stayed awake!"

As it ended, they huddled as a team, lifted helmets toward the sky, and shouted with joy! The coach yelled, "Only God could do this!" A player cried out, "I knew it would end the right way!"

It sounded so exciting! Too bad I slept through it.

It was not a co-incidence, but a God-incidence, that this was the verse I read in my devotional that day: Stay awake! Do not sleep like others! Watch and be serious! 1 Thessalonians 5:6 (KJV)

I began to think back to the Christmas Day that had just passed. I had just wanted it to be over. I was sick with pneumonia. My adult children were dealing with problems. It seemed there was little to celebrate.

As sad as it felt, I had been through enough hard seasons in life to recognize that difficult circumstances do not stop in order for me to have a 'good day' just because it is a special occasion.

We are going to have problems and struggles and disappointments in life - even on holidays - BUT GOD!

So, as we pray, it seems fitting to lift our hands toward the sky, let out shouts of joy, and say, "God, only You can do this! I know it will end the right way!"

Lord, I know You can do this! I may be in the battle, but I just need to stay awake, watch, and be serious. I know it will end the right way. Amen

The Good Shepherd

By Ann Farabee

One way to get into the spirit of Christmas is to see a Christmas play. There is the manger, Mary, Joseph, Baby Jesus, the wise men, the shepherds, angels, the star shining brightly in the sky to tell the world that a Savior is born, and on occasion even live animals.

Have you ever seen sheep? They are not clean. They are not white. They are not quiet.

When I was with my kindergarten class on a field trip to a farm, we saw some sheep. They were dirty looking and large, which surprised my students. Then, when one of the sheep emitted a true, "BAA!" they all backed away and huddled around me.
That "BAA" was loud!

Sheep have no survival skills, are dumb, feed from dawn to dusk, have poor vision, defend themselves by running, and they will follow other sheep off a cliff. They need a shepherd!

A shepherd watches over his flock, guides them, teaches them, searches for them, protects them, binds their wounds, nurtures them, cleans them, and provides a soothing ointment to comfort them when they are bothered by insects.

Those sheep. They sure are needy.
Those shepherds. They sure are good.

John 10:11 says that Jesus is the good shepherd, and the good shepherd will give his life for his sheep. He knows his sheep. He calls them by name. They know him.

The Good Shepherd - those are beautiful words.

It makes me want to look toward heaven, lift my hands in praise, and cry out to Jesus saying, "Baa…baa. I need You, Lord! Thank You for being my Good Shepherd!"

If we truly get a glimpse of how much the Good Shepherd loves and cares for us, we may not have to count sheep to get to sleep tonight!

I hope 'ewe' enjoyed reading this.

Lord, thank You for being my good shepherd. Thank You that You know me - and You call me by my name. Amen

Busy Busy

By Ann Farabee

I am busy right now. Those words easily slip out of our mouths, and the person wanting our attention walks away. We have all been there. Many times we say it to a loved one or family member.

We take care of the immediate, the necessary, the priority, and the important.

But in what order?
*   Immediate means nearest in time.
*   Necessary means required to be done.
*   Priority means most important.
*   Important means of great value.

We often tend to take care of the immediate and necessary before we take care of the priority and important.

In Haggai 1, the temple had not been worked on in 15 years. It needed rebuilding. Haggai read a message from the Lord to the people that included three very powerful words: Consider your ways. (KJV)

They had done the immediate and necessary, but not the priority and important. Good things…but not God things. Confused priorities could have caused them to miss the blessings of God.

But the Lord then stirred up their spirit and said, "I am with you." They then considered their ways.
They had been too busy being busy.
So, they went to work on true priorities.

Could we perhaps apply this to our holiday season? Yes, the Lord is with us. He will stir us up. Then, we can get to work on the most important Christmas priority - celebrating the birth of Jesus Christ, our Lord and Savior.

Lord, this holiday season, may I keep my focus on the birth of Jesus, who came to live on Earth, so He could shed His blood, die, be buried, and rise again so that I could attain the promise of eternal life in heaven. Amen

Light of the World

By Ann Farabee

For many, going to a Christmas play is a holiday tradition that helps us visualize the story of the birth of Jesus, so we can hold it more tightly in our hearts.

As a young teenager, I participated in a Christmas play at church. As an angel, my role was to stand near baby Jesus and hold my arms up in praise - like angels are supposed to do.

My heart was touched and tears filled my eyes, although at the time, I was not sure why. But, that night made a spiritual connection that has had a lifelong impact.

Now, I realize that the manger would have been a much darker place than portrayed in many Christmas plays. The shepherds would not be as neatly dressed. Sheep rarely look white - but grayish and dirty looking. The wise men did not visit baby Jesus until he was around two years old. When they did, they visited his home instead of the manger.

But that night after the Christmas play, as I stood in my front yard and looked up at the stars in the sky - I knew. I believed in Jesus. And maybe the star that was shining down on my life that night was the same star that was shining down on the manger the night Jesus was born.

Look up. The Light of the World is with us. John 1:5 says the light shines in the darkness, and the darkness has not overcome it. (KJV)

Gazing up at those stars became something I did often and I still do, for if the bottom of heaven is that beautiful, how much more beautiful will heaven be?

Lord, may I know that the story of the birth of Jesus is not just a story - but is HIS-STORY. Help me see the Light of the World and hold Him tightly in my heart. Amen

When Holidays Hurt

By Ann Farabee

For some - holidays hurt. I have been there too many times. I could not close out my devotions of encouragement without speaking to those of you who are hurting.

Sometimes, we do not look forward to a holiday.

We may have a broken heart.
We may have financial problems.
We may be sick.
We may be an addict.
We may be in an unhappy home.
We may be grieving.
We may be in prison.
We may be homeless.
We may be in the hospital.
We may not know where our children are.
We may feel there is no hope.

This list goes on.
Believe me - it is not just you.

You may be in a room filled with family.
You may be alone.
No matter where you are - you are hurting.
Those with you may know. They may not.

But God knows. God cares. God loves you.

In one of the darkest periods of my life that lasted for months, I was around others - but I was not really WITH them. I was grieving, hurting, and broken. It was as if a dark cloud was hanging over me.

I kept going. I kept doing everything I was supposed to do. Months later, I was sitting in church one Sunday, numb to what was going on around me, as usual. I looked up and saw a ray of sunshine coming in through the stained glass window. It shined directly on me. As it did, God sent these words into my heart, "I know you are grieving. I know you are hurting. I know you are broken. But the Son - and the sun - will shine on you again."

At that moment it happened. God healed my hurting heart.

Be still. Wait. Rest in Him. Trust Him.
He is a personal God - and He will send healing - to you.

Lord, send healing to those of us with hurting hearts. Amen

Joseph's Christmas

By Doug Creamer

Christmas is upon us once again. The packages are wrapped, the cards have all been sent, and the food is almost ready. Hopefully, we can stop all the rushing around and slow down long enough to savor this special time of the year. It's wonderful when we can set aside our differences and focus on what can unite our hearts, the birth of the Savior.

It's important to enjoy the traditions of this special time of the year. The special music, the familiar holiday movies, and the decadent desserts put everyone in the holiday mood. For some, the holidays wouldn't be what they are without all the shopping. For many, it's the Christmas parades that make the season. But I think we all enjoy those special Christmas programs at church.

My thoughts this year have turned to Joseph and the way he experienced the coming of Jesus. First, I imagine he struggled with doubt when he found out that Mary was pregnant. I imagine he felt sad and angry when he considered which of the local scoundrels had soiled his beautiful bride. The thought of losing a woman he was so deeply in love with must have been painful.

The Bible teaches us that Joseph was obedient to his dream from heaven. The angel told him the baby was God's son and to take Mary home as his bride. Even after such a powerful dream I wonder if Joseph struggled with doubt. I mean, who ever heard of a virgin giving birth? I believe the doubts may have intensified as they were in Bethlehem and Mary gave birth to her firstborn son.

I believe God knew that Joseph was struggling with doubt so he sent him three powerful signs to help alleviate his doubts. First, the shepherds come with an incredible story of angels. Two years later, the wise men arrive with incredibly expensive gifts. Finally, after Joseph escapes to Egypt, he hears that all the boys two years or younger living in the vicinity of Bethlehem were slaughtered.

100

I believe God saw Joseph as a man of great faith. I believe his carpentry skills were excellent. I believe he lived and worked with integrity. I think God believed in Joseph. He had hope that Joseph would raise Jesus in a godly way and teach his son good carpentry skills. I believe Joseph taught Jesus much about faith in the family, faith in the joys and sorrows of life, and faith in God when you are facing persecution.

I believe that Joseph taught Jesus that you must trust God even when you don't understand it all. I believe Jesus learned obedience to God from his father. I believe that Jesus learned the importance of waiting for God from Joseph, who guided his family safely to Egypt and back to Nazareth through prayer, listening, and obedience to God. Joseph was a good father to Jesus.

I believe that Joseph and Mary are very much like you and me. God had hope and faith in them. He hoped that Joseph and Mary would do what was right. He had faith in their parental abilities. He gave them a very important job to do. While I am sure that they were not perfect, they were faithful and fulfilled God's purposes.

I believe that God has the same faith and hope in us. He has given each of us talents and gifts and He wants us to use those abilities to bring glory to Him. He wants us to live with integrity in a world that is looking for the shortcut and the easy way out. He hopes that we will let our light shine in this dark world to offer His hope, grace, and mercy to anyone who would receive it. God has placed His hope in us as much as we have placed our eternal hope in Him.

I want to encourage you to consider the role that Joseph plays in the Christmas story. God saw in Him what He sees in you and me, the potential to do great things for His kingdom. God had faith in Joseph. Christmas is a lot of things, one of which is a celebration that God has faith in us. Jesus came to bring hope to a sinful world. At this time of year, I wish each of my readers the peace of Christ which goes beyond understanding, the love of God which is deeper than we can comprehend, and hope which will give us strength to face each new day with the joy of the Lord's birth in our hearts.

Trust His Heart

By Lynna Clark

Back in the days of yore before the internet, traveling was pretty much a crap shoot. We went with some friends to Gatlinburg in hopes of staying in a motel with a lovely view of the mountains. We pulled into a place all willy-nilly and hoped it would be nice. My buddy Ann commented that she'd be fine as long as it didn't include a pink toilet. Our standards back in the day were quite high.

Our husbands lugged the bags to our rooms and a short while later we checked on our friends. Though the toilet was a lovely shade of beige, their view was less than spectacular. However, they would be able to keep a close check on our vehicle as they had a panoramic view of the parking lot. David invited them to our room where the drapes were still drawn. He even offered to switch places with them as he described the beautiful setting out our window. Ann sat on the side of the bed while David opened the heavy curtains with a dramatic flair. We had a good laugh as we gazed at the side of a brick building. As usual, it's a good thing we know how to laugh.

I wonder how Joseph felt while hauling his plump little woman to Bethlehem. This normally small town was the home of his ancestors and probably Mary's as well. Tradition reveals that there was likely family dwelling there. Hospitality was a big deal in those days and good Jewish families often hosted travelers in their homes, especially if they were related.

I wonder why Joseph and Mary didn't stay with family. Was it shame? Did they get tired of the questions and suspicions surrounding their circumstances? Joseph and Mary were good people. They did everything God asked of them though it was incredibly hard. I imagine Joseph questioning the Lord as they checked into their smelly accommodations. I picture him apologizing to his wife and wishing that somehow he could provide better. I see this faithful man as he makes her as comfortable as possible then delivers a son that he knows is not his.

I read something profound the other day that made me think about this season in my own life. The writer said, "Christmas has never been about pretending everything is fine." –Monica Brands

102

Life is so hard at times. Friends and relatives may turn their backs. Others may point their finger and doubt our character. We may be tempted to pretend that all is well. The place we've found ourselves may include a brick wall or a dirty stable. Rather than question the plan of God, instead may we trust the One we've come to know as Faithful. Like the line from an old song says: "When you can't trace His hand, trust His heart."

The view will not always be lovely. But our wise and loving Lord has a plan.

And He can be trusted.

Tommy's Christmas

By Doug Creamer

The sun felt warm, but the air was cool from the rain of the previous night. The birds were taking advantage of the puddles that were left behind. They sang and splashed and enjoyed a cool drink. Children could be heard playing in the park, enjoying their first day of summer vacation. School was out and the joy of summer could not be contained.

The woman and the boy walked quietly along the sidewalk, their heads down and their hearts heavy. They each carried two suitcases, all the world had allowed them to own. Their pace was brisk, their thoughts cloudy.

The old, dilapidated house sat across from the park and lacked the joy of the children playing just across the street. The weeds were almost as tall as the first floor windows. The shrubs were no longer well-manicured, but rather, wild and untamed. The white picket fence around the yard was weathered. Its paint was peeling and it leaned like the earth was a magnet, pulling it down to the ground.

When they opened the gate it fell off its hinges and leaned into the tall weeds. The concrete sidewalk was the only thing protecting them from the encroaching weeds. They walked up the steps to the wooden porch that was worn and unappealing. They found Henry sitting in a rocking chair on the porch. He hardly noticed their approach.

"Hello, Henry," Martha said in greeting. "It's a pleasant summer day."

"Martha," he grunted laying down the paper. "Hello, Tommy. It's nice to see you."

"Hello, Uncle Henry," Tommy mumbled, with his face to the ground.

"What brings you two all the way over here?" he asked,

eyeing the suitcases.

"Tommy, why don't you run over to the park and play with the other children. Uncle Henry and I need to talk for a few minutes."

"Yes, ma'am." He walked slowly over to the park and rested on a swing. He didn't so much ride the swing as allow it to glide back and forth while he sat on it.

"Why is he just sitting on the swing and not playing with the other children?" Henry asked.

Martha looked over at him. "It's hard to play when your heart is so heavy."

"Why the suitcases?" Henry asked.

"Your sister's landlord gave us until the end of the school year. School got out yesterday, and he was knocking on the door at nine this morning, wanting us out."

"How kind," he picked up his paper and resumed reading.

"We need to talk." Martha pushed. "We have nowhere to go."

"I don't see why that's my problem," he said, while turning a page of the paper.

"She was your sister. Where else am I supposed to turn?"

"We got cousins. Why don't you check with them?"

"They're in Alabama!"

"So…"

"He needs to stay here. He needs his circle of friends if he is going to deal with his grief."

"By here, are you implying staying in my house?" he said, while laying the paper down.

"Henry, he needs to stay here with you. You are family."

"I don't want some kid in my house. Who is going to take care of him?"

"I could stay for a while, if that will help."

"Help? I don't know the first thing about raising a kid!"

"Look, we need to stay here for at least a few days until we can figure this out."

"So it's 'we'? You're not going to leave me alone with the brat?"

She nodded "Of course not. I'll stay until he gets settled or until we figure something out."

"Okay. You two can use the two rooms at the top of the stairs. There is one on the right and one on the left. There is a den straight ahead. You can use that too. You make sure that boy stays away from my rooms at the other end of the hall, and you keep him out of my study, which is down on the first floor. I don't want that kid bothering me while I'm working. If he gets in any trouble, you two will be out on your ear. Do you understand that?"

"Yes. I will take our things up to our rooms."

"Don't you touch anything else in the house, you hear me?"

"I won't." she said, picking up her things and heading for the door. She stepped into a front entryway filled with mail. It was stacked from the floor to the ceiling. There was a path leading to the back of the house and one leading up the stairs. Even the stairs had mail on them as she climbed up to second story. She opened the door to the first bedroom and could hardly enter for all the cobwebs hanging everywhere. She set the suitcases down and waved her arm to clear a path into the room.

Everything was covered in a thick layer of dust. She turned on the light and it barely cut through the darkness. The room smelled musty, like the door hadn't been opened in years. She didn't know where to begin, or even how. The heavy drapes concealed the window and any of the morning light. She made her way to the window and pushed back the drapes, which created another billow of dust and dirt.

The morning light tried to pierce the room but was stopped by the filth. She unlocked the window, and after wrestling a bit, was able to get it open. It was the first breath of air the room had experienced in a very long time.

She stood and looked around the room. The furniture was perfectly set in the room. The dresser had pictures that were carefully placed, but unseen through the dust. The bed held what might be a beautiful bedspread if one could remove the layers of dust that covered it.

Martha walked back down the stairs and out onto the porch. "What happened in there? There's enough dust and cobwebs to choke a horse."

"If you are unhappy with the accommodations, you can leave

if you like."

"That's not the point. It just needs a good cleaning."

"Be my guest."

"Where do I find supplies to clean up?"

"There's a closet at the top of the steps with some towels. Use some to clean and some in the bathroom. There is a washer and dryer next to the bathroom if you want to wash the sheets."

"Thanks. I think I will put the sheets in right away. What are we going to do for lunch?"

"There's a food truck that stops by and I'll get us something when it arrives. What about Tommy? What are you going to do with the boy?"

"Leave him over there for now. After lunch, he can help me upstairs."

Martha spent the rest of the day cleaning the bedroom and bathroom, which was in about the same shape as the bedroom. Martha and Tommy slept in the bedroom she had cleaned; she would start on the other bedroom in the morning.

The next day while Martha was working on the other bedroom, Henry came in and asked, "What is Tommy up to?"

"How should I know; I've been working up here since I got up."

"Well, he is doing something to the fence."

"Why don't you go ask him?" Henry didn't move so Martha got up and went to the door and looked to see what was happening. "It looks to me like he is fixing the gate."

"Who asked him to do that?"

"No one, he is probably just doing it to help out."

"Well, he should have asked before going in the garage and messing with my tools."

"Just be glad he is fixing it. We all deal with grief differently. Tommy tries to fix things and make things right. He lost control of his world, this is his way of getting some of that back." Martha returned to her cleaning. A little later Henry was at the door again.

"What is he doing now?"

"What's the matter?"

"He's out in my garage messing with my tools again."

"Why don't you go see what he is doing?"

"What will I say?"

"Ask him nicely what he is doing. You don't have to ask him about how he is feeling. Ask him if you can help. That might be nice." They walked to the window and looked out at the garage. They could see the lawnmower and Tommy working on it. "It looks like he is trying to get the lawnmower running."

"That old thing hasn't run in years. He'll never get it going. Why is he wasting his time?" Just then they heard the sound of a motor running.

"Sounds like he got the lawn mower going." Martha said and turned to return to her work. Tommy worked hard to tame the wild yard. When he finished, he had to rake the yard. It took most of the day. The next day he went to work on the weed eater and the leaf blower and got them running, too.

After Martha got the bedrooms, bathroom, and den cleaned up, she announced to Henry that she would get in the kitchen and see if she could make them a proper meal. He tried to stop her from going through the closed door, but she pushed past him.

She looked around and saw everything piled up. Dishes overflowed the sink. The cabinet doors were all open with nothing inside. There was trash piled everywhere. She looked and saw some mice that didn't seem bothered by their presence. She could see bugs crawling everywhere. There was one small path from where they stood to the back door. She looked at Henry in disgust. He held his head down.

"I've been meaning..." but he couldn't complete the sentence.

"This place is a disaster!" she exclaimed. "I wouldn't let a pig or any animal in this kitchen. Is this why you get take out all the time?" He didn't answer. He just stood there and stared at the floor. "It is going to take...days to clean this mess. I am not sure I will ever want to cook in this kitchen. Do you see the bugs and the mice? This is gross!" Henry turned and walked back to his study and closed the door.

Martha called Tommy in and they filled six green garbage bags with takeout containers, cans, and bottles. Tommy stacked the bags outside while Martha continued to fill them. She sent Tommy to the corner store to buy some dishwashing gloves, dish soap, cleaning supplies, disinfectant, and more trash bags.

Martha spent the next three days scrubbing and cleaning the kitchen. She ran the dishwasher over and over again. She disinfected all the cabinets and slowly began the process of putting things away. She spent half a day on the stove and another half day on cleaning out and cleaning up the refrigerator. She left nothing undone.

Once order had been restored, she went to the grocery store, filling two carts to restock the kitchen. That evening she made a roast with all the trimmings. They sat down together for their first home-cooked meal. Henry and Tommy ate with delight. When the meal was over, Henry looked at Martha and thanked her.

"And thank you for cleaning that kitchen. I know it was a god-awful mess. I am sorry you had to see it and clean it. I thank you from the bottom of my heart."

Martha smiled and looked at the two of them, "It was a labor of love. I love a good clean kitchen. It inspires me to cook. From the looks of things, I would say that dinner was a success."

"It was more than a success, it was delicious." Henry responded.

"I am glad you both enjoyed it."

"Um, hum." Tommy chimed in with his mouth still full.

"Tommy," Henry began, "would you like to make a little money?"

"Doing what?" he asked cautiously.

"Well, I was thinking of working on the shrubs around the house. You got the yard looking so good, they need to get trimmed up, too. Would you be willing to help me?"

"Sure," he managed, with a smile.

"Let's get started about 8:30 tomorrow. I will do most of the cutting. You can haul the stuff up front. The city will pick up limbs the day after tomorrow. You will need to stack things up neatly. I will show you where I want the pile."

They worked the whole day outside. They trimmed the trees and got the shrubs back in shape. The next day they worked on weeding the flower beds. Martha went to the hardware store and bought some bedding plants and mulch. When the boys finished one area, she moved in and planted some flowers and put the mulch down. When they finished the yard looked the best it had looked in years. They stood together on the front sidewalk and admired their work.

That began a series of projects around the outside of the house. They cleaned the gutters, did a little roof repair, and then painted the outside of the house. Martha helped from time to time, but mainly she stayed out of their way. Henry was teaching Tommy how to maintain a house. Tommy was drinking up the attention like a wilted plant.

By the time fall rolled around, the outside of the house was looking great. Tommy returned to school, and Henry to his teaching position at the university, but they continued to work on little projects together on the weekends. When the fall leaves came down, they raked them up. Henry made a big pile and allowed Tommy time to jump and play in them, laughing all the while.

In the meantime, Martha pushed her way into the living room. She found the newspapers stacked from floor to ceiling. It took her three days to bundle all the papers up and haul them to the recycling center. When she finally got the room completely cleared out, she asked Henry if she could paint the room. He bought her what she needed and she did a great job bringing the living room back to life.

Once she got that done, she decided to paint her bedroom and Tommy's room. Henry and Tommy caught the vision and painted the hallways and the dining room. By Thanksgiving, the inside of the house was beginning to match the outside.

Henry asked Martha if she would be willing to host some family and friends for Thanksgiving dinner. Everyone would bring dishes if Martha would make a turkey and a ham. She agreed. The gathering was a huge success. Everyone laughed and had a good time. The old house was feeling more like a home. Love and care were not only filling the house, but their hearts, as well.

On December first, they woke up to an early snowfall and canceled school. Tommy played outside the entire day, stopping only for a bite to eat. Henry locked himself up in his office for the day. He hardly spoke at dinner, and returned to his office after he ate.

For the next couple of days, Henry remained locked up in the office any time he was at home. When Saturday rolled around, he was still hiding in his office. Tommy slipped in to ask him a question.

"What do you want, boy?" Henry snapped, when he saw the intruder.

"I was wondering if we might get a Christmas tree."

"No, we aren't getting a dang Christmas tree. Now get out of here."

"But…"

"There are no buts about it. No tree!"

Martha heard the exchange and when Tommy left to go play with his friends, she went into the office to see Henry. "You were a little rough on the kid."

"What are you doing in here?" he snapped at her.

"I just came in to see what is going on. I thought things were going along pretty well, but now we are back to how you were acting when we first arrived. Do you want to talk about it?"

"Do I want to talk about it?" he mocked her. "No!" He turned his face away and stared at the computer monitor. He made no attempt to work or do anything. Martha stood there and waited. She just gave him the room.

After a few long moments he said, "I feel guilty."

"About what?"

"Laughing and enjoying your presence and…. Tommy, too."

"Why does that make you feel guilty?"

"I shouldn't be enjoying life. I feel like I am being unfaithful to my wife and son."

"It's been over two years. And if she was standing here right now, she would tell you it's okay to move on. It's okay to laugh, smile, and have some fun."

"How do you know what she would feel?"

"I met your wife once and I don't think she would want you to be miserable. Nobody wants that for someone they love. You or I can't change what happened. It was a tragedy."

"One day we are both living here in anxious anticipation of our son arriving. The next day I am a widow without a child."

"There were complications during the birth of your son and things went wrong. It's not your fault. She just slipped away."

"Leaving me here, all alone."

"You aren't alone any more. You have us."

"That's what makes me feel so guilty. I caught myself laughing on Thanksgiving. I haven't laughed since…"

"It's hard to let go, but you have to find a way. She would want you to be happy. Maybe the first step would be to remove the ring."

He stared down at his wedding band. It was all he had left to tie him to his wife. Tears streaked down his cheeks. He played with the ring. He slid it off his finger and held it in his hand. After a long moment, he slid it back in place.

"It's not easy. But you have to let her go. You have to give yourself permission to live, to enjoy life once again. You have been doing that with me and Tommy. We're here and we need you and you need us." Martha let that hang in the air. She quietly slipped out of the office.

Over the next couple of days Henry gradually reconnected with Tommy and Martha. By the following weekend, things had improved. Tommy asked about a Christmas tree again, hoping that Henry's better mood might grant him success, but no such luck.

Tommy's last day of school before the Christmas break arrived and Tommy was filled with mixed emotions. While he would be glad for the break from school, he was also disappointed that they would not be celebrating Christmas in Henry's house.

When Tommy left for school, Henry went into the kitchen to see Martha. "Can I give you a hand with the dishes?"

"Sure, I won't turn away help." He grabbed a dish towel and began drying and putting the dishes away.

"Have you got plans for the day?" he asked innocently.

She looked at him and smiled. "Nothing that can't be changed. Is there something I can help you with?"

"Well, ... I had this idea. I was thinking that maybe we could surprise Tommy. I was thinking of maybe getting a Christmas tree and getting it decorated before he gets home from school. I mean, if you would like to, I would appreciate your help."

Martha stopped washing the dishes and reached over to give him a hug. "That would be one of the nicest and best surprises we could give him. Yes, I'm in."

"I will go find us a nice tree if you will clean up a spot in the living room for it. I have some decorations, but maybe we could go out and find some new things. I think I want to get some new lights, too. We'll have to hurry to get it all done before he gets home from school.

"I was thinking that after supper I would go in and turn on the lights and then call him in for some reason. I want to get this old set of trains I have set up, too. We are going to have to work fast to get it all done in time."

"Don't worry, we'll get it done. This is going to be such a nice surprise for him."

"Do you think so?"

"YES!"

Everything was set before Tommy got home from school. Henry was in his office and Martha was in the kitchen when he got home. They acted like nothing had changed. Tommy played with his friends and came in when dinner was served. They shared a nice meal and talked about Tommy's Christmas party at school. When dinner was over, Henry pushed back from the table and asked Tommy "Did you know that I know how to play the guitar?

"No. I have never heard you play. I've seen the guitar case in the living room, but I never heard you play."

"Well, the truth is Tommy, I haven't played much for a long time. I started playing again the last couple of weeks in the afternoon before you got home from school. I left the guitar in the living room. How about you go fetch it for me and I'll play you and Martha a couple of songs."

"Okay." Tommy made his way to the living room followed closely by Martha and Henry. As he rounded the corner and entered the room, his eyes nearly popped out of his head. There in the corner was a beautifully decorated Christmas tree. He just stood in the doorway and stared at it. His face shone like an angel.

"Do you like it?" Martha asked. His mouth opened but no words formed. His eyes and face gave them all the answer they needed. Henry walked over behind Tommy and admired their work.

"You can go in and look at it a little closer if you like. The trains work too, if you want to run them." He ran over to the tree and immediately started running the trains. He played with them for a while. Martha put her arms around Henry and he put his arm around her. Suddenly, Tommy jumped up and ran over and hugged them both.

"Thank you! This is the best Christmas present any kid could ever hope for." Then he returned to the trains and played with the people and the village under the tree.

It was well past Tommy's bedtime when Martha came into the living room and told Tommy and Henry they needed to wrap it up for the night. Martha went upstairs. Tommy hugged Henry and thanked him again for the tree and the trains. Henry looked to be sure Martha was gone and then whispered to Tommy,

"We need to go shopping tomorrow. We want to find something nice for Martha for Christmas. Now don't tell her, it will be our little secret. We'll tell her we are going to the hardware store, okay?"

"Yeah, that will be great," he said with a huge smile.

The next few days passed quickly, as Tommy and Henry put some Christmas decorations up outside and Martha added some inside. They made some cookies and Martha baked some pies and a cake. The house was filled with the aromas of all the wonderful things that Martha was baking. The excitement grew as Christmas drew closer.

On Christmas Eve the three of them dressed up and attended a service at the Presbyterian Church just down the road. The stars were shining brightly as they walked home. The air was crisp, but not too cold for a winter evening.

The Christmas lights were beautiful on that peaceful evening. Each house was decorated differently. Some had candles in the windows, while others had lights outside. A few houses had enough lights to light up an entire city. Tommy stopped in front of those houses and stared in amazement. The lights seem to twinkle in his eyes.

Tommy stopped in front of their house and stared at the lights. They had icicle lights hanging from the gutters. They had colored lights in all the shrubs along the front of the house. Through the living room window he could see the Christmas tree all lit up. His eyes danced with excitement as he anticipated Christmas morning.

The three of them stood silently out in front of the house for a few minutes. Somehow the peacefulness of Christmas had found a way into their hearts. The bells from the Baptist Church began to play the sweet melody of "Silent Night."

"I better get in. I have a few things to do before I turn in." Martha said. She walked up the sidewalk, leaving the boys out at the street.

"I am not sure I thanked you," Henry broke the silence, "for all the work you have helped me do around here. The house looks the best it has in a long time. Most kids your age don't care to help out around the house. I just want you to know that I appreciate all that you have done."

"I live here too, you know." Henry laughed. "I want it to look nice, too." Henry put his hand on Tommy's shoulder. Tommy looked up at him and smiled. They stood there another moment, admiring the lights on the house and the sweet melody from the church.

"Well, we better get in there. Did you wrap the presents we got for Martha?" he asked as they walked up the sidewalk.

"Yes, and I put some pretty bows on top."

"Good. You go and get them and sneak them under the tree. I will make sure Martha stays busy in the kitchen."

"Got it." And Tommy ran up to his room to retrieve the gifts and placed them under the tree. While he was there, he took the opportunity to shake a few of the packages with his name on them. Henry and Martha sneaked a quick peek of him. They smiled and returned to the kitchen.

Tommy went to bed and tried his best to sleep, but the excitement of Christmas was overwhelming. He woke up at five and eventually fell back to sleep until six-thirty. There was no going back to sleep then. He knew that they had agreed to get up at seven. Tommy stared at the clock, willing it to move faster. Time crept slower than a snail.

Finally, the clock read seven and Tommy ran into Martha's room. "It's Christmas! It's Christmas! Get up!" Martha rolled over and enveloped Tommy with a big hug. "Come on, there is no time for that. We need to get down there and open the presents."

Tommy leapt from the bed and was running out the door to get Henry up. As he turned the corner he ran straight into him. "Well, what's all the excitement about?"

"It's Christmas!" Tommy exclaimed.

"Christmas? I was thinking about some coffee and my breakfast."

"Are you kidding? There are packages to open down there!"

Martha slipped into the bathroom while Tommy and Henry made their way downstairs. Tommy plugged in the Christmas lights and Henry put on some nice Christmas music. Tommy ran up the stairs to check on Martha's progress and then was back in the living room. Martha made it to the living room just before Tommy tore into his first gift.

Tommy opened some of his gifts and then Martha suggested they take a break to get some breakfast. With a few things to enjoy, Tommy conceded. Henry went out to the garage and Martha went to the kitchen. Within a few minutes, there was a nice breakfast on the table. Tommy gobbled his food faster than lightning. Martha excused him to go back to the living room while she and Henry finished up.

After breakfast they returned to the living room and finished exchanging gifts. Henry and Tommy gave Martha some gifts, and then Martha and Tommy gave Henry a few gifts, too. Tommy ripped through the rest of his gifts, enjoying each one.

When all the packages had been opened, Henry returned to the kitchen and refilled his coffee mug and brought some for Martha, also. Henry and Martha sat and watched Tommy enjoy his gifts. There was laughter and joy in the house, something that had been lacking in all their lives.

As Martha and Henry finished their coffee, Henry asked Tommy if he would mind going out to get him the morning paper. Tommy moved slowly away from his gifts to head out the front door. When he had opened the door and stepped out onto the front porch he stopped in his tracks. There on the front porch was a brand new bicycle. Martha and Henry were standing at the door watching Tommy's expression, which was priceless. He stood and stared at it and then he walked around it, allowing his fingers to caress the seat and handlebars.

"Well," Henry asked, "do you like it?"

"Yes. Is it really mine?" he asked with eyes filled with wonder.

"I don't think Martha and I can ride it, so yes, it's yours."

"Wow! It's awesome! Can I go for a ride?"

"Yes," Martha said, "but first, put some clothes on."

Tommy raced to his room and was back downstairs with lightning speed. He and Henry went outside to enjoy the new bike. Tommy road around close to the house and Henry seemed to be enjoying the experience just as much as Tommy. Henry retreated to the warm house while Tommy went for a long ride around the park and community.

Martha stood watching out the window. Henry joined her and they both enjoyed seeing Tommy race up and down the street.

"Thank you for making this such a wonderful day for Tommy." Martha said as they returned to the living room.

"I think I enjoyed it as much as he did. It sure is nice having the two of you here."

"We're glad to be here, too. Thank you, again."

"I am glad that Tommy is out riding around for a minute, I have one more gift for you."

"What?"

"Yeah. I...uh...wanted a minute to talk with you." He cleared his throat. "I have to tell you that I sure have enjoyed you two being here with me. You...have helped me come out of a very dark place in my life. You have helped me to live again. I can't remember when I laughed or even smiled before you two came into my life."

"Then you look around this house. Wow, it looks so much better. We have painted everything and you have helped clean up the yard. You have brought life to me and to this house as well. You helped make this house into a home. You have no idea how much I appreciate it."

"In fact, I might say that you two rescued me."

"Oh, I think you rescued us. But remember, you almost didn't let us in."

"Oh, what a mistake that would have been. This house would still be a terrible mess and me, well, I would be in worse shape than I could imagine. It's because of the two of you that I have found a way to live again."

"With that in mind, I want to know if you think we could make this a permanent arrangement. I want you and Tommy to stay."

"That is very nice of you. I know Tommy will be happy. I will see if my old room is available where I used to live when I worked for your sister. This is going to be great for Tommy."

"I don't think you understand me properly. I want you to stay, too."

"Oh, that's very kind of you. But, I think it is probably time for me to go. I will find employment somewhere. I am sure you will give me a good reference." She said with a laugh. "That will give you and Tommy time to grow closer together."

"No, I want you to stay, but I don't want you to stay in the

117

capacity of being the maid." He reached into his pocket and pulled out a small box and presented it to Martha. "I want you to stay in a different capacity." He had the biggest smile on his face that Martha had ever seen. She looked at his hand and could only imagine what might be in that small box.

"Are you asking me to…" she covered her mouth.

"Yes, I am asking if you will do me the honor of being my wife."

Martha stared at the box and then looked deeply into his big blue eyes. They seemed to be dancing with excitement and love. She took the box from his hand and opened it. There was a beautiful diamond ring inside. It took her breath away.

"Me?" she asked.

"Yes, Martha, you. You brought life and hope back into my life. How could I ever let you get away? So, what do you say?" She looked at him, then at the ring, and finally back at him.

"Yes, nothing would make me happier." They embraced and then they kissed for the first time. "What a wonderful Christmas day." She whispered in his ear.

"I agree. There is only one more thing that will make this day complete."

"What is that?"

"I want us to be a family. I want to see if Tommy will let me adopt him."

"Are you sure?"

"Yes. The adoption papers are sitting on my desk. I just don't know how to ask him."

"We'll do it together." She said, embracing him so hard she nearly took his breath away.

A little later Tommy came in from riding his bike. His cheeks were red from the cold and he was breathless from the fun. He went into the living room and played with his toys.

Martha came down stairs. Henry was in the office. She tapped gently on the door. "Shall we go talk with him?"

"I'm nervous."

"Don't be. I think things are going to turn out fine. Come on."

They walked into the living room together and sat on the

couch, watching Tommy play with the trains under the tree. The moment was peaceful.

"Tommy," Martha broke the silence, "can you turn off the trains for a moment? We would like to talk with you."

"Sure," he said bringing them to a halt. He sat up across the coffee table from them.

"Tommy, we want to share a little news with you," Martha continued. "Henry has asked me to become his wife," she said, looking back into his big blue eyes. "And I said, 'yes'"

"Does that mean that you are going to get married?" he asked.

"Yes, that is exactly what it means." She said.

"Wow, that's great," Tommy said.

"Tommy, there is something I would like to ask you," Henry began. "I am so happy that Martha has agreed to become my wife, but I want us to be a family."

"It feels like we are a family." Tommy said.

Henry smiled big and looked over at Martha, who nodded and winked. "I am glad to hear you say that, Tommy. How would you like to make that official, us being a family?"

"What do you mean?"

"I would like to adopt you." Henry said.

"Adopt me? I thought you already had."

Henry laughed. Martha began to cry. "So, to clarify, you would like us to become a family?"

"I thought we were, but if we are making it official today, then this will go down as being the best Christmas ever!" Tommy jumped up and threw himself into Henry's arms. Martha reached over and made the family hug complete.

****

Family is a place where you belong. It's the place you call home. It's being with people you love and with people who love you. Family looks different for each of us. Some of us are family with those who are biologically bound. Others discover family with people from completely different backgrounds. Family can be found in the place where you live or among a group of people who love and care for your wellbeing, like your church family.

Home is sometimes the place where we grew up and sometimes it is it the place where we find ourselves now. Home can be defined by the people we are closest to and by the food that we eat what makes us feel warm, loved, and accepted. Home can also be defined by certain aromas. Maybe it's a certain food being cooked or maybe a scented candle or even the smell of the sheets when you climb into bed.

I believe home is more like a feeling. We feel loved. We are around familiar things. We are with people who share common expressions. We are understood. We aren't judged. We are encouraged and challenged to be the best version of ourselves as possible.

Home is a place we all long to be. Tommy found home among people who were not his own. He is loved, well fed, and deeply cared for. That's why I believe our spirits all long to go to heaven. We want to be with our God and Father who loves us, will take good care of us, and will lead us to our everlasting home.

Jesus came into the world as a little baby born in a manger. He was far away from His home. But He came to show us THE way home. He pointed to the way, led the way, and opened the doors to the way home. I encourage you to open your hearts and to find your way home. Come join the family of God where you will always know you are on your way home. The gift of God, eternal life...living at home in heaven...is available to all. Don't you want to come home and be a part of the best, loving family of all?

It's the best Christmas present of all, Jesus, born in your heart, filling you with love, making you a member of the family, and leading you to your eternal home in heaven.

Beautiful Joes

By Lynna Clark

What could he do? It came down to a couple different options. He could break their engagement and tell everybody she'd been unfaithful. Or he could handle things quietly in order to protect her. Being a nice guy he chose option 'B.' He would cancel the wedding plans and somehow move on without her.

Suddenly an option was presented to him that he'd never considered.

He could marry her and raise the baby as his own. It would include taking a hit to his reputation and trusting a woman with a very questionable story but...

Matthew 1:19 tells us that Joseph was a good man. Even a good man would struggle with option 'C.'

Isn't it remarkable that the King of the universe chose to come to earth as a man so that God's beautiful plan to buy us back to Himself could be realized? To me it's interesting that **He started and ended with a couple of regular Joes.**

The first was just a hardworking, tax paying guy looking forward to having sons of his own and building the family carpentry business. He found himself being the adopted dad of a little boy Who would be revealed as the Son of God. But Joseph **willingly gave up reputation** and whatever it took to protect this child. When it meant believing a far-fetched story about his fiancée, he was willing. When it meant taking off to a foreign country with his brand new family in tow, he was God's man.

Good, faithful, hard-working, steady Joe; not much by social standards, but chosen by God.

Fast forward to the end of Jesus' life.

Another Joe steps up. This time it's a rich man with great social status. But he refused to accept the verdict of his fellow religious leaders who had wrongly convicted Jesus. With wisdom he stepped out from the Jewish high counsel and made a decision. He would personally take the body of Christ and bury it in his own tomb… the one he just paid good money to have carved out for himself. This rich man with great social standing did not ask servants to do the difficult task. He made his request to Pilate, then took the body of Jesus and carefully wrapped it in fine linen, placing it in his own tomb. **What courage! He could've lost everything by associating himself with Jesus.**

Instead, he is forever chronicled in Scripture as Joseph from Arimathea, a good and righteous man.

Two Joes: One poor, without clout; the other rich, with high social standing. **Each faithful, steady and strong in character, just doing life as the Lord guided.**

In my life, the people who have influenced and encouraged me most have not been dynamic, flashy, or extremely talented. **They have been beautiful though,** because faithfulness is a beautiful thing.

Don't you love how God uses us regular Joes for His most important tasks?

PS: You can read more about **Joseph the step-dad** in Luke 2:1-24 & Matthew 1:18-2:23; and **Joseph of Arimathea** in Luke 23:50-56 & Matthew 27:57-61.

The Gift

By Ann Farabee

It is beautifully wrapped. It has your name on it.
It was sent to you by someone that loves you.

Even though the gift is free and given willingly, we must receive it and open it.

We just look at it. We talk to others about it. We wonder what it is. Those around us finally say, "Why don't you just open it?"

If we did not open it, not only would we miss out on our gift, but how would the giver feel when offering a gift that we would not receive?

John 3:16 - For God so loved the world that He GAVE His only begotten Son, that whosoever believes in Him should not perish, but have everlasting life. (KJV)

Yes, God gave His Son so that we could have eternal life... Now, that's a gift!

Ephesians 2:8 - For by grace are we saved through faith; not of ourselves. (KJV)
It is the GIFT of God.

The gift of God? Yes. It is free. We can't buy it. We can't earn it. We don't deserve it.

John 4:10 - While Jesus ministered to the woman at the well, He said, "If you only knew the GIFT of God." (KJV) If we understood the magnitude of His gift to us, we surely would not waste one second receiving it.

God gave us a gift. It is a personal gift.
He reached down from heaven to deliver it to us.
He sent His Son, Jesus, to bear the sin of the world on the cross.
The world? That is you. And me. It is all of us.

Because God loves us, if we don't immediately accept the gift of salvation when He nudges our heart, He usually keeps gently pushing it toward us, reminding us that the gift is still available.

I received my gift years ago, and it is the best decision I ever made.
If I could receive and open your gift for you, I would. But - I can't.
Because it is your gift. It is from God - to you.
Go ahead…open it.

Lord, may I receive - and open - Your gift to me. Amen

Christmas is Almost Here!

By Doug Creamer

Christmas is almost here. Hopefully the shopping and the cooking are almost done. My tradition for most of my life includes wrapping my gifts on Christmas Eve. I know I am looking forward to spending some time with family and friends, getting some extra rest, and having time to reflect on 2016.

I am also looking forward to the Christmas Eve service. Our pastor's mother had a vision for the service. She felt led to create 100 Christmas stockings to be given out to needy families during the service. I could not imagine how it would happen. Then I walked into the sanctuary the other day and saw 100 hand knitted, filled stockings hanging along the front of the church. I couldn't believe how wonderful and magical it all seemed.

My pastor and his wife have worked to identify some children who will be getting very little for Christmas. They sent personal invitations to those families and called them to make sure they are coming. In a very real and tangible way, we want to bring the spirit of Christmas to these families. We want to offer them the hope that Christ offered us when he came as a little baby born in a manger.

I find it difficult at times to hold onto my faith, hope, and God's unconditional love when everything goes crazy during the holiday season. There are so many commitments to be here and go there. The demands on my time feel overwhelming. This year has been different. This year I have determined I will live in the moment, no matter how crazy the Christmas season feels. I have often wondered what it was like for Mary and Joseph to live in their moment. A required trip to Bethlehem couldn't have come at a worse time. Imagine arriving in town only to discover there was no room left in the inn. Then, to make matters worse, the baby chooses that moment to come into the world. Mary needed shelter and help; where were they going to go and what were they going to do? Where was God?

We can't always see God working behind the scenes. We don't always understand His plans or purposes. All we can do is take one step at a time and know that He has made good plans for our future. Joseph must have questioned everything as Mary struggled to bring Jesus into the world. How could he be the father to God's son when he didn't provide a good place for them to have the child? Whether it was a stable or a cave, it was no place for God's son.

Joseph must have decided to stay in Bethlehem for at least two years because that is how long it took the wise men to arrive. Joseph worked to build his business and reputation in Bethlehem and then shortly after the wise men leave, God tells them to move again. How could that make any sense? Trusting in God and His divine plan required faith.

We celebrate the arrival of our Savior as a joyous occasion, but for Mary and Joseph it was a day-by-day struggle with faith. Their journey to raise our Savior required that they trust God in impossible circumstances. They had to listen for God's voice and live obediently. Sometimes God's provision was miraculous, other times required hard work. They had to trust a loving God to meet their needs, to know their circumstances, and to believe that He was watching out for them.

Mary and Joseph had to trust God every step of the way, especially since they were raising His son. They didn't always understand everything, they had to have faith. They knew more than anyone else that God loves us because He sent His son into the world. They knew the power of hope because their child was the hope of the whole earth. They knew that faith could pull you through dire circumstances as theirs had done over and over again.

I want to encourage you to open your hearts to God's love. Jesus came to the earth so we could know that God loves us. We can trust God with our future because we know He is creating it out of His love for us. The path we will follow will require faith, but having faith in a good God should be easy. I know that I can look at tomorrow with hope in my heart because Jesus came and died for me. Christmas is all about having faith in a God who loves us and who is planning a hopeful future for us. God bless you and Merry Christmas!

Roasting O'er an Unlit Fire

By Lynna Clark

So what's the deal with all the humidity? Nobody dreams of a damp Christmas… or a sticky New Year. We actually broke down and turned on the air conditioner lest the heat wafting off the relatives cause tempers to flare. Some of us of a certain age cannot be overheated without dangerous consequences. Men take note: when a woman picks up a magazine or a church bulletin or a dishtowel to fan herself, it's time to turn on the air. Never mind that it's winter; there's nothing jolly and bright about a sweltering woman in room full of guests.

Nobody dared light candles or God forbid build a fire in the fireplace. Ambience was no longer the goal and festive lighting dropped waaayyy down on the list. Keeping mama cool was the number one concern, at least for any man who considers himself wise. Take my husband for instance. Christmas is over and the ceiling fans are still spinning at warp speed. THANK YOU DARLIN'!

Our grown kids made footprints of the three youngest grands at some point in yesteryear. Fashioned from salt dough they are always on display. However lately they're more like sponges. The indentations of their tiny feet began to drift slightly. So into the oven they went. The peanuts in the fruit bowl became a little wiggly as well and had to be toasted again too. Therefore the oven was set to 200 degrees for an hour. They were still a little chewy when we checked them; [the peanuts, not the footprints.] It was sort of like biting into a raisin when you're expecting something crunchy. T'was a little disconcerting. So we roasted them another hour while I made our traditional holiday salmon stew.

I called to my beloved from the kitchen. "Turn the air down another notch honey. I'm still hot."

"Yes baby you are," he replied. I fanned with a dishtowel and gave him the look. It wasn't pretty, but it WAS HOT.

The salmon stew was perfect except for the heat of it. We fanned and slurped it down like we had good sense. Why ditch tradition just because El Nino is passing through. Certain things must always be done after the holidays; like washing Christmas socks, and discovering that last snowman on top of the refrigerator, and apparently consuming salmon stew.

"Lord have mercy! I'm dying!" I exclaimed as we finished our late supper. A window was flung open which allowed a warm breeze to enter the kitchen... a very warm breeze. I walked outside in my pajamas no longer caring what the neighbors thought... bless their hearts. Immediately my hair multiplied like fluffy bunnies forming a lovely cotton candy look around my glowing face.

Again, not pretty... but it WAS HOT!

My beloved joined me and we took that opportunity to haul Frosty and his miserable companions to the building out back til next year. Water ran through the yard as it had reached its limit. I understood. Mud marred up past the black line on my favorite Converses. But a little breeze stirred the balmy night air delivering a moment of reflection.

"At least our heating bill won't be as high as last year." One of us spoke hopefully.

The other one of us wisely observed. "Yeah... but we'll make up for it by running the air conditioner full blast."

We walked back to the house through the nature induced sauna. A piney wreath laden with fake snow smiled at me from yet another door. I decided I like it there... at least til spring. That's probably when we'll get a record breaking snowfall.

Maybe then I will finally cool off.

My Favorite Christmas Songs

By David Freeze

Do you ever hear those people complain when the stores start playing Christmas music the day after Halloween? Well, I don't mind at all.

In fact, a few Christmas carols in July wouldn't bother me. I love to sing along with them, something not easily done because I can only carry a tune in a bucket that some would prefer to put over my head.

My singing is terrible, but who really cares? My sixth grade teacher, Mrs. Briggs, used to have us line up like a chorus and sing on Wednesdays. She would go around and listen to the individual singers and if they were hurting the overall sound, they got to go sit down. Nearly every Wednesday, I got to enjoy the songs from my desk with a red face.

Until Christmas time, that was. For some reason, my voice must have been better when we were singing Christmas songs. Maybe she was just a little more kind then. Either way, I do love those sings.

Honorable mention — There are so many great Christmas songs; 11-15 are favorites too, but for some reason, my top 10 just seemed a tiny notch better. Numbers 11-15 are "The Most Wonderful Time of the Year" by Andy Williams, "Christmas Time" by Stevie Wonder, "All I Want for Christmas is You" by Mariah Carey, "Merry Christmas Darling" by the Carpenters, "So This is Christmas" by John Lennon or Celine Dion, and anybody good doing "Away in a Manger." I just snuck an extra one in.

No. 10 — "I Saw Mommy Kissing Santa Claus" by the Jackson 5. Michael nailed it in this version released in 1970. It is easy to imagine a young Michael really excited at Christmas.

No. 9 — "Wonderful Christmastime" by Paul McCartney. One of the top worldwide favorites, McCartney performed the song first in 1979 and last did it publicly on Saturday Night Live last week.

No. 8 — "Christmas in Dixie" by Alabama. Alabama was one of my favorites and this song mentions Charlotte, Caroline and celebrates Christmas all through the south. It was first released in 1982.

No. 7 — "Blue Christ-mas" by Elvis Presley. I don't think Elvis ever made a bad song. I love his gospel and Christmas music, and it was a fact that Elvis most enjoyed that music too. Elvis first recorded the song in 1957 and claimed it as his own favorite Christmas song. There is a great version with Martina McBride doing a duet with Elvis in one of those retro voice overs.

No. 6 — "I'll Be Home for Christmas" by the Eagles. Sometimes called "Belles Will be Ringing," it was released in 1978. Martina McBride had a version that topped the country charts and is also one of my favorites. Yes, I really like Martina.

No. 5 — "Old Toy Trains" by Roger Miller. It was re-leased in 1967 about a little boy wanting to wait up for Santa and dad urging him to go on to bed. I love to play and sing this one, picked by Nashville as one of the top 50 country songs of all time.

No. 4 — "White Christmas" written by Irving Berlin in 1940 according to most accounts. No one is really sure where or exactly when Berlin wrote it. White Christmas, sung by Bing Crosby, is the largest-selling Christmas song of all time according to the Guinness Book of Records. I'm already excited that the forecast on the weather radio is calling for snow flurries on Christmas morning.

No. 3 — "Silver Bells" was first sung by Bob Hope and Marilyn Maxwell in the 1950 movie, "The Lemon Drop Kid." It was originally named "Tinkle Bells," but thankfully that didn't last long.

No. 2 — "O Holy Night" composed by Adolphe Adam in 1847. My top two songs are obviously my favorite traditional songs, but I especially love the "O Holy Night" versions done by Josh Groban and Mariah Carey. It is easy to listen to both of these and remember the real reason we celebrate this season.

No. 1 — "Silent Night" written by Franz Gruber in 1816. This song absolutely means Christmas to me, and makes me have chills when I hear it done well. Some of my favorite renditions are done by Elvis Presley, Amy Grant, Neil Diamond and Nat King Cole.
This is just my list and I thought it would be fun to do. Most likely, I'll have one of these songs on my mind well past the big day. There is a good chance that I might be heard singing one of them too. Cover your ears, or better yet, feel free to join in.

The Bumpy Ride

By Lynna Clark

"Oh no! What about the J-turn?! Y'all do NOT want a Jeep! Those things turn over way too easy." That's what my mama heart cried when our daughter Stephanie and hubby Jeff bought their first new vehicle. They were so excited. Lots of adventure was in their future! They'd get safari hats and bandanas and hit the road with the top down. Somewhere in the far reaches of my brain was tucked an article about the dreaded J-turn. All I could think about was the Jeep tipping over if they took a corner too fast. Then one day they showed up at my door and Jeff took me for a ride. OH HOW FUN! Next thing I know I'm shopping for bumper stickers that say, "Hang on! Let's try something new!"

On New Year's Day I asked the Lord for help for the coming year. Again I requested that He turn things around for us. You see, we've just finished one whole year without employment. One. Whole. Year. No unemployment benefits, no regular paycheck, just God's blessings as needed. It's been a very slow process and quite miraculous. Many people have been so good to us. "Give us this day our daily bread" has been answered day by day, month by month, until finally the year is finished with all bills paid.

Instead of a quick fix, He's taking us on a wide berth it seems. No J-turns. I guess He knows we'd likely get dumped on our pointy heads. So slowly but surely our path is directed by His kind shepherding heart. No whip. No scolding. No driving of His sheep. Just a gentle still small voice.

Sometimes my heart feels like screaming "Just get on with it already!"

But He doesn't.

He's the Shepherd.

I am not.

Here's the prayer I prayed way back in January 2013, before David lost his job the following fall. From Psalm 69:14-17: "...pull me from these deep waters... answer my prayers, O LORD, for Your unfailing love is wonderful. Take care of me, for your mercy is so plentiful... don't hide from Your servant; answer me quickly, for I am in deep trouble!" (NLT) In the margin I wrote, "Please turn things around for us Lord. We need a miracle." I dated it 1.7.13 and went back to it often to remind myself to trust Him. I remember feeling like the water was up to my nose as I stood on my tippy toes trying to catch a breath.

Later that year our house would be foreclosed on and all the equity we built in our forty years of marriage was lost. Our lawyer advised us to file chapter 7 bankruptcy to protect us from crazy new tax laws. Skin cancer added to the fear, financial burden and embarrassment. Job and ministry loss followed.

But here we are.

Neither of us has gone hungry… obviously. We live in a cute little house just right for the two of us. The doctor got all the cancer and my nose grew back. There's even toilet tissue to spare.

OH. MY. DEAR. SWEET. LORD! The wonderful provision and care You've given us is amazing! "Many will see what the Lord has done and be amazed! They will put their trust in the LORD." –Psalm 40:3b (NLT)

And that's why I'm sharing our troubles… for without trouble, there's no need for faith. When we can do it all ourselves, why ask God for help?

So we look to Him and trust, "You crown the year with a bountiful harvest; even the hard pathways overflow with abundance!" –Psalm 65:11 (NLT)

As we enter the new year I feel the Lord reminding us to stay strong. We answer, "Yes Lord! We've travelled a bumpy road before. But would You PUH-LEEEEZE watch out for the J-turns?"

We grab our hats and jump in. I feel the sun on my face and His smile as He seems to say,

"Hang on! Let's try something new!"

Hope

By Roger Barbee

The pandemic rages across every level of world lives. Even isolated villages and towns now feel its presence. In the United States we are a few days from electing another cycle of government leaders, including a president, while European leaders try to make hard decisions to combat the virus. We are bombarded by noise that is masked as news worthy information. The editorial in our local paper today asked: "Are you tired of...?" and then went on to list many of the noises we have be subjected to during the pandemic and its affects.

Yes, we are tired, but we have quite a distance to travel. In a marathon, racers train to be able to maintain pace and form during the last 6.2 miles, the crucial last miles which begin at mile 20. Metaphorically that is where we are: Mile 20 of a marathon and where our preparation and resolve will now be tested.

As a teacher of literature, I always chose to expose students to stories and poems and novels and plays that taught a lesson. A brief poem such as Earl carries a lesson that, once learned, will help in difficult times that we all will encounter. Like the well-trained marathoner, a well-read person will have an arsenal to call upon during tough times as now. Having digested such great literature as The Odyssey, a person can use lessons gleaned from Homer's words to help him or her to carry on; to "Get on with it," as the English haberdasher told me one summer in his store on Oxford's Turl Street. The list of such literature is long, but sadly forgotten it seems to me. But that is another matter for another essay.

Like all people, I am tired of the turmoil and the uncertainty of this pandemic and our dithering leaders. However, a retired man of 74 living with his wife, five cats, and two hounds on Lake Norman, I have had to cope with only some inconvenience, but nothing like that of a parent with school-aged children and a job or, worse, not a job. These people are facing a difficult circumstance which I am happy not to have to navigate. But I still was reminded of the poem Ithaca by C.P. Cavafy this week because of the death of Sean Connery and his connection with the poem, and the lesson it carries for us during the pandemic.

Sir Sean said years ago that his big break came when he was five years old, but it took him seventy years to realize that. The break he told of was that he learned to read at age five, and reading then changed his life, opened doors, gave him insight, and more. He said, "It's the books, the reading, that can change one's life." 007! Bond! James Bond! He was a reader. He read newspapers, books, magazines. He devoured it all, changing his life.

I knew none of this until my wife, after reading an obituary of Sir Sean, shared some of it with me, especially the above quotation. He was a man after my heart, but I was aware of one instance of his reading and it is a fine example of literature, of reading and how that changes lives. And it is right there on the You Tube channel. Type in "Sean Connery and Ithaca" then listen to him reading the words of Cavafy. Hear the music of Cavafy's phrases and allow their meaning to become part of your soul. See the visuals and hear the canned music, but most of all allow Cavafy, through Connery's resounding Scottish accent, assure you that the trials we face during the pandemic are just another part of a journey we face, and they, and it, too shall pass. Allow Cavafy's lesson to give you comfort that you, like Odysseys and us all, can gain Ithaca, our safe harbor, our restful home.

Happy New Year

By Ann Farabee

My New Year's Eve memories:

My early years were most likely spent at home. Does that count as a memory?

For at least 10 years as an adult, New Year's Eve was spent in church, where we worshipped until past midnight, while my children slept on the carpeted floor of the church. This I remember! These are great memories!

Four New Year's Eve celebrations, dating back to 1986, were spent with my acquaintance - Pneumonia.

Many years were celebrated watching the ball drop in Times Square - on television.

In recent years, I discovered that the new year will arrive whether I am awake or not, so I go to sleep prior to midnight.

My funniest memory of New Year's Eve: My 18 year old daughter went on a date to celebrate the arrival of the year 2000. They surprised us by arriving home at 11:45, and I still remember the look on her date's face when he told us he wanted to be home with us in case Jesus came at midnight.

We all want a Happy New Year! A new year gives us new hope! It gives us a fresh start. We try to be of good cheer, although we know we will face problems in our lives. John 16:33 says that in the world, we will have tribulation, but we can be of good cheer - for Jesus has overcome the world. (KJV)

Can all our years be happy? Yes. We can live beyond our circumstance. If we find joy in our hearts, inward peace and everlasting contentment will be there, too.

Lord, may I live for you to a greater level than I ever have before! Thank You for being with me in the past, in the present, and in the future. Amen

Happy New Year!

By Doug Creamer

The packages have been unwrapped. The bows and ribbons are scattered. The stockings have been unhung from the chimney with care, emptied, and the treats have tickled our taste buds. We are all rubbing our full tummies wondering how on earth we ate all that food. The tree still sparkles in wonder and the lights outside continue to help hold back winter's dark night.

Many have determined their gifts do not fit so they are off to the shopping centers to exchange them. Others have hit the stores hunting for bargains to snatch up with their gift cards. Still others are finding wrapping paper and cards which will safely be stored for next year.

Soon we will all begin the task which I hate…putting Christmas away. I enjoy getting the decorations out, but I absolutely do not like putting the Christmas things away. But here we stand just a short time until the New Year begins. We still have a little time to enjoy some family, friends, and a little more good food before the doldrums of winter roll around.

It's an odd time but a good one. We have the privilege to reflect back on the year that is about to end and the opportunity to imagine what the New Year will bring our way. I assure you that each one of us has had some good memories that we will cherish and if life has been normal in your house there are some memories that you would rather forget. We have to choose which memories we will carry with us and which we need to leave at the threshold of this New Year. Some things we need to let go so we can move forward.

Some believe we should never look back at the past but I think differently. I have discovered after a lifetime of looking back on my last week in order to write a column that looking back allows me to see the hand of God in my life. I don't know about you, but sometimes when life seems to go crazy, it is hard to see God in those moments. It takes time and distance to be able to look back and see the hand of God moving and acting on our behalf.

137

I believe that reflecting back on life and looking for God's hand builds our testimony to His goodness in our lives. We need to be able to tell others about the goodness and faithfulness of God. Our journey is our story and our story can be the very thing that helps others who are struggling. So now that the holiday season is drawing to a close, look back on how you lived life this year and how God worked in and through you.

Each of these memories you choose to treasure and carry with you into the New Year will be a blessing for you and for others. As we turn our eyes to focus on the New Year I hope we can see the future with positive possibilities. We need to believe that God is making good plans for our New Year. We know that there will be good days and bad days, but we want to look for God's hand as He guides us through each one.

I believe God is blazing a trail for us, planning new adventures. God wants to see us grow spiritually strong so that means there will be some challenges waiting in the New Year that will help us develop spiritual muscles. God wants us to be closer so He will be waiting for us where we have our quiet time. God wants to pour more of His love, grace, and peace into our lives so the opportunity to receive more is waiting for us in the New Year.

God sees a future that is hope-filled and bright. God sees a future where we are walking in His grace. God sees a future that goes beyond our imagination. God sees a future where we, His sons and daughters, are living in peace and fulfilling our God-ordained purposes. God sees a future where churches work together to reach the lost with His love.

I want to encourage you to take a few moments to reflect on the good things from this year that is ending and to prayerfully consider God's good plans for your future. We know God is good and that He is planning good things for our future. With joy we will close this year and with faith we will enter the New Year knowing that God is good, faithful, loving, and waiting there for us.

Happy New Year!

ABOUT THE AUTHORS

Doug Creamer retired after 34 years of teaching. His last 18 years were spent at East Davidson High School. Since he retired, he is teaching Chinese students English over the internet. He writes a weekly column that appears in four newspapers. His books include Encouraging Thoughts, The Bluebird Café, and Revenge at the Bluebird Café. He lives with his wife in Salisbury, North Carolina where he can be found outside working in his yard if he isn't working on his website, www.EncouragingU.com or writing.

His website is: www.dougcreamer.com/
Email : doug@dougcreamer.com

Author **Lynna Clark** loves the simple things in life and especially humor. After surviving breast cancer, she says each day feels like a gift. "Just being able to enjoy food and coffee and the ability to function is a wonderful thing." She and her husband David of forty-six years live in Salisbury, NC.

Books include the Blue Meadow Farm series of five; Too Far Gone; Hope Angels; The Weakest Reed; and Just a Little Cancer Journey. All books are available at Attractions on Main in Salisbury, NC, Missions Pottery & More in Lexington, NC and on Amazon.

For articles like those written for the Salisbury Post, please visit her blog site at www.LynnasWonderfulLife.wordpress.com . Her aim in life is simply stated in 1 Thess. 4:11, NLT:

"Make it your goal to live a quiet life, minding your own business and working with your hands, just as we instructed you before. Then people who are not Christians will respect the way you live and you will not need to depend on others."

Ann Farabee, from Kannapolis, North Carolina, is a writer, a columnist for the Faith section of the Salisbury Post, a ministry speaker, and has a passion for prison ministry, as well as those trapped in addiction.

She has worked as a youth leader, in children's ministry, Sunday School teacher, Praise Team leader, women's ministry leader, and directed the ECHO drama team, as part of Passion for Purity ministries.

She taught 35+ years in Kannapolis City Schools and Mooresville Schools, having taught grades K-8. She also worked as system wide math coordinator in Grades K-4. She graduated from UNC-Charlotte, is a National Board Certified Teacher, has a Master's Degree in Education, and has been Teacher of the Year and Time Warner Cable All-Star Teacher. She has also served as past president and vice-president of the Kannapolis Bible Teaching Association.

She is a mother and grandmother, and is married to Charles Farabee, who is owner of Charles Farabee, CPA, in Kannapolis.

She loves sharing her story with others to encourage and help strengthen them in their walk with Christ. Find out more about Ann at annfarabee.com or contact her at annfarabee@gmail.com.

David Freeze - An accomplished runner and endurance cyclist, David Freeze discovered his love of writing during graduate school. David has written eight books that include various solo long distance cycling trips, a run across North Carolina and a year-long odyssey aboard a historic biplane. Now with over 90,000 running miles including 24 marathons and over 20,000 endurance cycling miles covering all 50 states and Canada, David often weaves his love of fitness into his writing.

A free-lance writer for the Salisbury Post and various other publications, David owns a small farm near Salisbury, N.C. and is a personal trainer and motivational speaker. He believes that ordinary people can accomplish extraordinary things. David has two daughters and one granddaughter and can be reached at david.freeze@ctc.net.

Roger Barbee is a retired educator living on Lake Norman in North Carolina with his wife, five cats, and two hounds. His words have appeared in the Washington Post, the Birmingham Arts Journal, Page & Spine, Memoir Magazine, Potato Soup Magazine, Ailment, and other print or on-line publications. He is a regular contributor to The Sports Column and encouragingu.com. You may reach him at rogerbarbee@gmail.com

M. D. Cox created the cover illustration and design for this book. His gift and help have been such a great blessing.

M. D. Cox is an illustrator base out of North Carolina. He is inspired by the curiosities of the world around him, permeating through his passion for traditional mediums like ink and watercolor.

Follow him on Instagram:

https://www.instagram.com/m.d.cox/

Made in the USA
Columbia, SC
17 November 2020